ONE MAGICAL CHRISTMAS

When Annie Berry collides with Nik Knoll in a car park on the day of her sister's wedding, it feels like all of Nik's Christmases have come at once. Annie seems just the sort of woman he'd love to get to know, and the chance nature of their encounter is almost like — well, Christmas magic. But Nik has a secret, and he has to be sure that he can trust Annie before he tells her . . .

BERNI STEVENS

ONE MAGICAL CHRISTMAS

Complete and Unabridged

LINFORD
Leicester

First published in Great Britain in 2018 by
Choc Lit Limited
Surrey

First Linford Edition
published 2021
by arrangement with
Choc Lit Limited
Surrey

*A catalogue record for this book is available
from the British Library.*

ISBN 978–1–4448–4764–2

Published by
Ulverscroft Limited
Anstey, Leicestershire

Printed and bound in Great Britain by
TJ Books Ltd., Padstow, Cornwall

This book is printed on acid-free paper

*For everyone who loves Christmas
as much as I do.*

Acknowledgements

'We think you should write a contemporary Rom Com,' said my publisher. 'A Christmas contemporary Rom Com.'

'Er . . . I said.

'With no vampires.'

And just like that, the gauntlet was thrown. (Actually, is the gauntlet ever thrown these days?) You know what I mean anyway. It was a challenge.

Christmas is a very special time of year for all sorts of reasons, but I especially loved the years when my son, Sam, believed in Santa. It made everything feel so magical, and because he believed so whole-heartedly, he almost had me believing too. The memories of those years set me thinking . . . what if . . . ? This story grew from there.

So my thanks firstly have to go to Sam for his belief in magic and his love of all things fantastic, because my inspiration came from the Christmases of his childhood.

I also have to say thank you to my friend Suz's daughter, Holly, and just mention that their surname isn't the same as my heroine's. Not quite.

To the fabulous Choc Lit Tasting Panel — thank you for liking Nik and thank you for enjoying the story. It means a lot to me. Special thanks to the Panel readers who passed *One Magical Christmas*: Megan C, Jenny M, Lucy M, Vanessa W, Yvonne G, Gill L, Carol F, Jo L, Cordy S, Els E, Nancy S and Joy S.

Massive thanks to Choc Lit themselves, for encouraging me to stray from my usual gothic path, and out into the light for a change. And thanks as always to my very patient editor, who helped me stay in the light, and for reminding me every now and again that it was Christmas.

Last but by no means least, thanks to my husband Bob, for feeding me and supplying the occasional beer during the editing process. I couldn't have finished this book without him!

1

August

Early August and London is dusty and sweltering. A heat haze shimmers above the road and pedestrians' tempers are frayed. Horns blare from angry black cabs, and the tourists saunter along Oxford Street at nought miles an hour, stretched across the pavement as if they have all the time in the world. Which to be fair, they probably have. *They* are on holiday.

Unfortunately for me, it's Thursday, and my day off. I'm desperate to find an outfit for my sister's wedding which is only six weeks away. My *younger* sister's wedding, I should add. Shouldn't there be a rule about younger sisters *not* getting married before older sisters? Will there be sympathetic glances my way on the big day? I'm only twenty-seven, but still . . .

I need to find something to wear that

says, 'young and trendy and really not at all desperate to get married'. Which I'm not. Desperate to get married that is. Although I do feel the need to start looking for the right outfit early, rather than leaving it to a mad, stressful dash the week before. Who knows what horror I might buy if desperation kicked in?

I decided to have a look in Selfridges, even though most things would be way over my budget. A veterinary nurse doesn't earn a huge amount after all, but there's no harm in looking.

I crossed over the road and glanced in a couple of other shop windows on my way to Selfridges It certainly looked as if autumn had arrived in force. No doubt there'd be Christmas jumpers in all of the windows soon. I love Christmas, don't get me wrong, but I prefer it to stay in December where it belongs. It just doesn't seem right looking at anything festive in sweltering summer heat. Although once the first of December arrives, I'm probably one of the most festive people on the planet.

When I reached the main door of Selfridges, I noticed a sign advertising the fact that their Christmas store was indeed 'now open on the lower ground floor', and sighed. Christmas really does get earlier every year. If that all sounds a bit 'bah humbug', then your name isn't Holly Berry. Yes I know — hilarious isn't it? Luckily for me, my middle name is Anne, and throughout my school years I switched to Annie, which I've used all the time since. My parents clearly have a weird sense of humour. Or maybe they simply didn't realise about 'Holly' and 'Berry' at the time, although I don't believe *that*. I do believe they have no idea that my name also sounds like a famous Hollywood actress — and you can just imagine the disappointment everywhere, when *I* turn up.

My younger sister — the beautiful perfect one, you know, the one who's getting married in October — is called Katie, which suits her and doesn't sound like a tree with red berries. She's lucky.

I wandered listlessly around the third

floor, looking at various dresses and suits with price tags like telephone numbers. What a way to spend my day off. I could have stayed home or read a book in the local park instead.

It's my own fault for wanting to get the perfect outfit in plenty of time. But I really like the idea of a gorgeous dress or suit squirreled away in the wardrobe just waiting to be worn. It will also mean I can remain relatively stress-free during the lead-up to the big day.

Then *the* dress almost waved at me. Sleek, midnight-blue and gorgeous. Feeling almost magnetically drawn to it, I touched the material with the reverence I normally save for pedigree Persians. I looked at the price tag, which was affordable — although barely. It was my size too, and instinctively I knew I would not be leaving the store without it.

'Would you like to try it on?' A smartly dressed shop assistant swooped in like an elegant vulture. I just nodded, and followed her to the changing rooms.

The dress fitted perfectly, and I felt like a movie star. I'd worry about paying the bills some other time — this dress had to be mine. Now there would be no way any ageing relatives would see me as the spinster sister stuck on the shelf. Not while wearing *this* dress. And it wasn't black, so the parents would be relieved.

Barely ten minutes later, I stood outside the store, feeling slightly lightheaded but triumphant, and clutching a huge yellow carrier bag with *the* dress swathed in tissue inside. Mission accomplished. *Eat slugs, disbelievers*. Annie Berry will be a force to be reckoned with at this wedding.

2

Nik sighed. Three missed calls from his father. Again. He knew what it would be about and didn't feel much like continuing the same old conversation.

He scanned the room with thoughtful grey eyes, watching several overexcited three-year-olds pinging around as they waited for their parents to collect them. He grinned at little Tom and his friend Danny, who'd been in the dress-up box again. Both were wearing long dresses and laughing at each other. Tom had even found an oversized handbag. Actors in the making for sure.

'How dare you allow my son to wear a dress?' An angry voice demanded, and he turned to see Danny's mother, immaculate as ever in her navy business suit, crisp white blouse and skyscraper heels.

'They're only playing, Mrs Jessop,' he said.

She swept towards her son without further comment and told him to take 'that thing' off at once.

'Like Mummy,' said the little boy, his bottom lip trembling.

'It is *not*.' The irate woman pulled the dress over his head, which prompted a flood of tears, and Tom instantly joined in.

Nik felt a tide of frustration sweep through him. He went over to the sobbing Tom, and picked him up, dress and all.

'They were just playing,' he said again quietly. 'No harm done.'

Mrs Jessop shot him a poisonous look. 'His father won't agree. If this ever happens again, I will move Daniel to another nursery.' Grabbing Danny's hand she stalked out, dragging the still sobbing child behind her. Talk about overreacting.

Soothing Tom, whose sobs had now calmed down to hiccups, Nik felt relieved when he saw Tom's mother — late as usual — rush in.

'Sorry,' she panted. 'Tubes are bonkers tonight, signal failure at Finchley Road.'

'No problem Mrs Evans,' said Nik, smiling as Tom wriggled free to reach his mother.

Unlike Danny's mother, Mrs Evans grinned down at Tom. 'Hey, nice dress Tommy!' She poked him playfully in his tummy. 'Bit long on you though.'

'Danny's Mummy was cross,' said Tom.

She looked up at Nik. 'No surprise there,' she said. 'Arms up Tomster, let's see if we can get this off and give it back to Mr Knoll. He might need it.'

Tom giggled and Nik joined in with the laughter. What a difference. He felt sorry for little Daniel.

Once free of the long green dress, Tom reverted to being a cute three-year-old boy. He swung on his mother's hand. 'Home Mummy.'

'Yes SIR. Say good night to Mr Knoll.'

'Night Uncle Nik,' said Tom.

'Goodnight Tom. Have a great week-end.'

'You too,' mother and son chorused.

Nik watched them leave. Now if he could find someone like Mrs Evans, he wouldn't mind getting married. He sighed. Fat chance. Women like that were rare and almost always taken.

His phone rang. Thinking it would be his father again, he didn't bother to check the caller ID.

'Dad?'

A girlish giggle stopped him from saying anything else. 'Hardly. It's Lucinda.'

His heart sank. 'Oh hi Lucinda.' He knew she would ask him about the vacancy at the nursery. Again. He regretted ever mentioning the job to a mutual friend in the pub one weekend. He'd agreed to interview Lucinda, and there was no doubt she had the relevant qualifications, but there was just something niggling away at him. He prided himself on being a good judge of character, and although Lucinda appeared to be friendly enough, there was still that indefinable something setting off alarm bells.

3

September

My dress passed the parental scrutiny — with flying colours actually. My mother's relief at the dress being something other than black was almost palpable. My father huffed a bit and said he'd thought I would be in jeans and wellies. I replied if it had been left up to me, I would have been.

Then I felt mean. It could have been much worse. Katie and Jon could have been going for the full church malarkey and then I'd have had to be bridesmaid — or, God forbid — the *matron of honour*, and forced to wear a meringue-style dress in a colour not of my choosing. Thank heavens for small mercies. I think the fact Katie and Jon are both designers is the reason they prefer the elegant and understated, and I'm relieved they do.

Katie literally squealed with delight when she saw the dress, and I felt pleased to have made everyone so happy. I can't afford to buy anything more exotic to eat than baked beans for a couple of months, but everyone *loves* the dress.

The wedding day was now hurtling towards us like an out of control express train — only three weeks away. September had kind of sneaked in, pretending to still be August. The days were warm and leaves were hanging on to the trees without even turning colour. My mother was stressed and uncommunicative, my father was keeping out of her way and I was on the look-out for a smart jacket to wear over the dress in case the weather suddenly turned cold at the beginning of October. I didn't think my ancient Barbour would quite cut it somehow.

Katie had taken to regularly whooshing in and out of my tiny flat like a whirling dervish. She fired questions at me that I had no hope of ever answering. Questions about flowers for instance. *How would I know?* Mum was dealing with things like flowers, and she didn't seem to be sharing information with anyone.

One particular evening Katie appeared again, her pretty face streaked with tears.

Horrified, I pulled her inside. 'What on earth has happened?'

'The wedding is *off*,' she said dramatically.

'Don't be a dingbat,' I said with customary older sister bluntness. 'Why?'

'Because Jon is an unfeeling, sarky . . . *prat*.'

'Well he *is* a bloke,' I agreed. She burst into tears and I led her into the living room. 'Sit.' I ordered.

I went to make coffee and grab a box of tissues.

Once she was at the gulping stage, I managed to wheedle what had happened out of her. As I suspected, it was nothing too serious — he wasn't having a mad passionate fling with a pole-dancer (have I mentioned my lurid imagination?) But it did appear he lacked tact and diplomacy when it came to commenting on Katie's appearance just weeks before the wedding.

'He thinks I'm *s-s-scrawny*,' wailed Katie.

'I'm sure he doesn't,' I said, casting an envious eye over my sister's perfect figure.

'He said I was looking a bit skinny, and then he said Hester in accounts is really curvy.' You have to admire the man's flair for self-destruction. What an idiot.

'Chesty Hester, eh?'

Katie laughed and hiccupped at the same time.

The doorbell rang, and no prizes for guessing who would be there.

'Don't let him in.' Katie clutched at my arm.

'Why? Is he dangerous?' I rolled my eyes and made a mock scared face. 'Stay in here, I'll talk to him.'

I opened the front door, and was confronted by a sheepish-looking Jon. 'You're a prize bozo,' I told him.

He nodded. 'I know.'

'Not content with criticising Katie's appearance, you have to comment on some other random woman's figure. What exactly is *wrong* with you?'

'I'm sorry.' He looked wretched, but I

wasn't done with him yet.

'There is no point apologising to me. Katie wants to call the wedding off, and quite frankly I don't blame her.'

He looked even worse. 'I love her so much. I don't know why I said that. She's perfect. But she has been going on about her appearance non-stop for weeks and I just flipped a bit.'

I eyed him sternly. 'She's the bride. She's very important.'

'Can I talk to her?'

'Wait here.'

I nearly fell over Katie, who'd obviously had her ear pressed to the living room door.

'Do you want to speak to him?'

She gave me doe eyes. Of course she did. I nodded, and went back to Romeo on the doorstep.

'Go on in, but don't be long. There's a new police thriller on TV in fifteen minutes.'

He gave me a grateful smile and scurried into the living room like a good future husband.

14

I sighed and shut the front door. The kitchen for me then. *Now where did I put those chocolate biscuits?*

I needn't have worried. The pair of them came out of the living room within five minutes of Jon going in, hands clasped, and with happy goofy smiles. Ain't love grand?

'Thanks Annie,' they chorused as they left.

'Pleasure.' I felt at least two hundred years old.

The place felt quiet without them, so I put the TV on, and slumped on the sofa — with the biscuits — ready to watch a new 'psychological thriller'.

There's nothing like a good old-fashioned murder. Just what the doctor ordered, so to speak . . .

4

Nik sat in the Dog and Duck nursing a pint of Old Familiar. It didn't taste very familiar. It tasted flat and warm, but definitely old. He wished he'd bought a bottle of beer now. At least it would have been cold, and possibly even have bubbles. He toyed with the idea of going to get a bottle anyway — he probably had time. Then he started to wonder if his date would show. He blamed his father. Trying to find the perfect girl in time, and one who pleased his family, seemed an impossible prospect. He hated deadlines — it was one of the reasons he'd started his own business.

Online dating. Ridiculous. Anyone could post a photo online and say it was them, couldn't they? There were warnings in all the newspapers about things like that. Although to be fair, the warnings were generally aimed at teenage girls and not grown men who should be able to look after themselves. His mind veered off into the unknown and simply terrifying. This woman could be seventy years old at least, or an axe murderer. A sudden picture of his potential date's post flashed into his head. He tried to remember the exact wording. *'Jemima: age 27, blonde with blue eyes. Occupation: Magazine editor.'* That didn't sound so bad did it? The accompanying picture had been a little blurred, but she'd looked okay.

He gulped a large mouthful of warm Old Familiar and very nearly choked on it when a quiet voice said, 'Nikolaas?'

He looked up and swallowed the mouthful of beer. Well, to be fair, she wasn't seventy. Possibly on the cusp of twenty-five — at the most — but she didn't look blurred or very much like her photograph.

'Er . . . sorry . . . are you . . . ?'

'Jemima, yes.'

'Puddleduck' instantly sprang to Nik's mind. Too many hours of reading Beatrix

Potter to the kids at the nursery. Still she looked nice enough, and she also looked very nervous. He felt a bit sorry for her. Standing up, he pulled a chair out for her.

'What can I get you to drink, Jemima?'

'Diet Coke please.'

'Coming up.'

He gave her his friendly smile as opposed to the special smile he reserved for someone he fancied. Although he wondered whether there was much of a difference these days, seeing as he hadn't actually met anyone he really fancied for quite a while.

When he came back with her drink and a decent bottle of cold beer for himself, she was sitting with her hands folded in her lap, staring into space. Most young women would have been glued to social media on their smartphones by this stage.

'So . . . you're a magazine editor, Jemima?' He gave her another of his friendly smiles.

She nodded. This wasn't going to be

easy. 'Which magazine do you work for?'

'*Knitting OK!*.'

Well if there was one thing in the world Nik knew absolutely nothing about, it was knitting. His mother didn't knit, neither did his father — as far as he knew. In fact, he didn't know anyone who knitted.

'And — er — do you knit?'

She actually smiled. It was a quick, very shy smile, but she smiled. 'Oh yes, I knit a lot.'

'What are you knitting at the moment?'

'Prince Harry and Meghan Markle.'

That wasn't the answer he'd been expecting. 'Sorry . . . what?'

'Everyone in the office is knitting a member of the Royal Family, but I was lucky enough to get Harry and Meghan on their wedding day.'

'Erm — congratulations?' He had no idea whether congratulations were in order, but it seemed appropriate somehow.

She positively beamed. 'Thank you. I'm *so* excited.'

There then followed a detailed explanation of needle sizes, patterns and the many different wools needed for Harry and Meghan. Nik tried to keep his eyes wide and interested, but found his thoughts drifting away.

'Do you mind if I ask you something?' He came back to earth with a bump, when he realised Jemima was asking him a direct question.

'Of course, ask away.' He hoped she didn't want to knit him.

'Do you have a drink problem?'

'A drink problem?' He felt flummoxed by that. Did he look like he had a drink problem? Sound like he had a drink problem? He didn't think so. He ran a nursery, and there were rules about people who worked in childcare, and he was very careful to abide by them all. He couldn't afford anyone to think he had a drink problem.

She gestured at the pint of Old Familiar and the bottle of beer Nik was currently swigging from. Ah.

'That beer was a mistake.' He pointed

at the offending pint, and gave a sheep-ish grin. 'I thought it would be good, but it's really not.'

She didn't look convinced.

'Can I get you another drink?' He half stood up, but sat back down when she shook her head.

'No thank you, I have to go.'

Nik wondered if he was being dumped already. He glanced at his watch, and saw it was only nine-thirty.

'So soon?' he said.

'I have an early start tomorrow.' She held her hand out and he shook it, feeling slightly bemused.

'Can I give you a lift home?'

She looked positively horrified.

'Oh I don't think you should be driving,' she said, pursing her lips. 'Perhaps you can get a taxi. My dad is picking me up in five minutes.'

Her dad?

Nik wished her good night and watched her weave her way to the door. Well that had been . . . different.

* * *

So *that* was online dating — a bit of a minefield. He didn't think he'd venture online for a while. Not even for his parents.

He gave Jemima a ten-minute head start, while he finished his bottle of beer. Then he left the offending pint of Old Familiar for anyone brave enough to drink it, and went outside to the pub car park, feeling a huge sense of relief when he reached the safety of his car. When he reached the outskirts of town, he began to see the funny side. He'd just picked a rubbish agency, he felt sure there must be better ones. *Bona fide* companies. Companies who actually met their clientele and could match people properly. He should have realised by the paltry joining fee, that 'Hearts United' weren't going to be any good. Stupid name anyway. Perhaps he'd do a bit more research when he got home.

5

October

One of the joys of being the 'non bride' is apparently being sent here, there and everywhere to check stuff. I'd checked the flowers, the buttonholes, the venue, the cake and the taxis.

Somewhere I'm sure I've read this is the duty of the best man. Now I have no idea why Jon would choose a lazy louse with an ego the size of a planet for his best man, but choose him he has. Katie says they're good mates, although I'm sure Jon has better mates. Am I being unfair? Maybe. Probably. Chris Jones, for those people lucky enough not to have met him yet, is the town lothario. Or he thinks he is. He leaves a scattered trail of broken hearts wherever he goes. But for some reason, he really *does* appear to be a good mate of Jon's. They are nothing alike, I hasten to add. My future brother-in-law — apart from his recent bout of tactless behaviour — is a real sweetie, and dotes on Katie. But his choice in best men, leaves a lot to be desired in my humble opinion. What makes Chris better than any of the other men coming to the wedding? It doesn't say a lot for any of them if he's the best. All he's done so far is collect the rings and write a speech — and I only have his word for it that he *has* actually written a speech. I'm pretty sure it will be rubbish anyway. There's more humour in a puddle than I've ever noticed in Chris. Actually puddles can be very funny — if you jump in them really hard.

I had a mental picture of splashing in a puddle all over Chris, and that made me smile. Don't feel sorry for him, he's a serial womaniser. Luckily for me, I've never been taken in by him, which is probably why he avoids me.

I'm really relieved the wedding is finally happening, because I really don't think any of us would survive another week. My poor mother is virtually gibbering, my father retreats behind his paper for hours — some say days — and I find myself checking things for the wedding that I've already checked at least twice. Katie is floating along on a cloud of blissful happiness, and I could slap her. She appears oblivious to the bedlam all around her, and apart from the slight hiccup a few weeks ago, is ecstatic about everything. Even at Chris Jones being best man.

However, I've always loved getting my hair done. Having an expert person shampoo, condition and style my hair, is the best de-stresser *ever*. Today, Katie and I are in the salon together. She's chattering away at a rate of knots, and I answer her in monosyllabic fashion, which she doesn't notice of course. This is her day, and I really *do* love having my hair done. I can feel the tension leaving my body. All is good with the world.

Two hours later, Katie and I are beautified — not that Katie needed too much help, or much make-up. I, of course, have an errant spot which decided to make a guest appearance on my chin.

Could have been worse, I suppose, it could have been on the end of my nose. Luckily the wonderful person in charge of our make-up has cleverly disguised said spot.

My dress is definitely the best part, without question. The moment I put it on, I feel like a million dollars, which isn't surprising, considering it cost the equivalent of three months' salary.

Katie whooshed in, and I stopped breathing for a moment. My little, and very annoying sister looked like a fairy princess. How could she be all blonde and super-model waif-like, when I have the unruly dark hair and slow metabolism? Life is very unfair sometimes.

'You look sensational,' I said, going over to hug her. 'Absolutely breath-taking, and if the bozo doesn't treat you like a princess, I will personally hunt him down.'

She giggled. 'You are funny Annie.'

'Yeah, funny Annie that's me,' I agreed.

But not in this dress. In *this* dress, I'm anybody I want to be. Rock star, film star — dancer extraordinaire.

I catch a glimpse of myself in the mirror. I don't look like me today, and there's a certain indefinable something in the air, which makes me feel different. If I believed in magic, which I don't, I would say something very special is going to happen today. Anyone would think it was *my* wedding.

I smiled at my reflection, or rather I smiled at the stranger pretending to be me in the mirror. The stranger smiled back elegantly. Yes, this was definitely going to be a good day. I could *feel* it.

6

Nik loaded his shopping into his car. He slammed the boot shut, and stopped to watch a wedding party leaving the town hall. The bride looked like a princess from a Disney film, all flowing blonde hair, shimmering dress and wide blue eyes. A fairy-tale wedding.

On cue, his phone rang.

'Dad, hi.'

'Nikolaas, how has your day been so far?' His father's deep voice boomed in his ear.

'Well, it's Saturday, so I've been food shopping, and now I'm going home.'

'Do you have plans to go out?'

'Possibly . . . ' Nik had learned over the years to be vague when talking to his father about his social life. It meant more questions, which inevitably ended with the one about why he hadn't found the 'right girl' yet.

'Will there be girls there?'

'No Dad, I'm going to a party in a monastery.'

'Sarcasm is the lowest form of wit, Nik.'

Nik sighed. His father usually had a better sense of humour than this, but lately he seemed to have lost it. 'Sorry,' he muttered.

'No, I'm sorry. I have a lot on my mind at the moment.'

'Anything I can help with?'

'I might need your help here next month, if you have any spare time.'

'Sure. Just let me know.'

'Thank you. Have fun tonight.'

'Thanks.'

Nik put the phone back in his jacket pocket. He felt worried about his father, and wondered whether he might be ill. Perhaps he should ask his mother. Except Dad was never ill. His health was ridiculously good. But something definitely wasn't right — he was never usually this short-tempered. Perhaps a discreet call to Mum would be a good idea.

His gaze drifted across to the wedding party again. He wondered if everyone in the party was impossibly good-looking, or whether they just appeared that way to him because he felt — if he was honest — a bit lonely. He turned to get in his car and had the breath knocked out of him when a vision in midnight-blue cannoned into him and knocked him to the ground.

'Oh I am . . . so . . . sorry.' The vision screeched to a halt, and he looked up into a pair of eyes that matched the dress. 'Can I help you up?'

That would have been funny if Nik had possessed enough breath left to laugh. The vision didn't appear either big enough or strong enough to lift a teacup, in spite of appearing quite tall, she looked reed-slender — especially in that dress.

He scrambled shakily to his feet, and gave her a smile. 'It's fine. I'm fine.'

She gestured across at the Disney bride. 'My little sister's just got married, Mum's having a cry and nobody had the sense to bring any tissues.'

Nik opened the boot of his car again and fished out a new pack of tissues. One of the bonuses of working with kids.

'On me,' he said.

'I . . . er . . .'

'*Annie!*' came a shout from over the road, which made the vision turn around.

'Thanks so much . . . ?'

'Nik. And you're welcome.'

He watched her rush back across the road. Luckily for the unsuspecting British public, she didn't knock anyone else down en route. Now why couldn't he meet someone like her online? She couldn't knock him down online either. That was a plus.

Another impossibly good-looking man emerged from the town hall, and took hold of the vision's arm. She was spoken for. Well of course she was. Women who looked like her didn't run around unattached. Not for long anyway.

Nik sighed. Too much parental pressure weighed on his mind. Perhaps he should go and see the folks more often.

It might stop the constant phone calls and questions about his private life. Not that he actually *had* a private life at the moment. In fact they'd probably stop phoning him if he did.

The wedding party were all piling into the waiting cars now, and he tried to catch another glimpse of the vision in blue. He spotted her in a car behind the bride and groom with the good-looking man. Lucky him. She suddenly looked out of the car window across the road at him, and waved. He grinned, feeling like a besotted schoolboy, and waved back. He grinned even more when Mr Handsome had a look too. Obviously he wasn't *that* secure. Feeling mischievous, Nik gave him a cheery salute and got into his car. Well that was his excitement over for the day.

* * *

Katie simply glowed. There was no other word for it. I truly have never seen anyone so happy . . . and *glowy*. If I wasn't so pleased for her, I'd probably feel sick. As younger sisters go, she's pretty okay. When we were little, she was a total pain of course. But she's all right now. Mostly.

I watched her and Jon mingling with the guests. Their happiness positively radiated out of them.

Then I noticed the odious Chris pursuing one of Katie's friends; possibly the only girl in town he hadn't managed to date yet. Apart from me. And we all know *that* will never happen. How I'd restrained myself from socking him one when he'd grabbed hold of my arm outside the Town Hall, I have no idea. In my defence, I think I'd been happily day-dreaming about the dishy blond guy I'd knocked flying in the car park. He'd been so nice about it too. Even donated a pack of tissues to the weepy mum cause. Of course, no doubt he was blissfully married with loads of kids. Hunks like him don't grow on trees. Not the nice ones anyway. Hunks — not trees.

The reception was a lot of fun. I'm more than happy to get on the dance floor, I always have been. Of the two of us, most people think Katie would be the confident dancing type, but she really isn't. I was the one who insisted on having dance classes from a very early age. In fact dancing is very possibly the only feminine thing I've ever been interested in. My hatred of dolls is well-known in the family. Nasty, creepy things. Of course this could have been a result of watching Dad's old video of *Barbarella* when I was far too young to watch it. Imagine being trapped in a room with hundreds of dolls with sharp teeth. It gave me nightmares for a week. I think mum threw the video out after that.

'Penny for them, Annie.'

I turned around to see Chris smiling his oily smile.

'I was mentally wishing you luck with your latest conquest,' I said, matching his oily smile with a sarcastic one.

'Jealous?'

'*What?*'

'If you noticed, you must be jealous.'

'I was bored mostly, but not as bored

as I am now.'

I left him standing there, trying to work out whether he'd been insulted or not, and went back on the dance floor. If in doubt — dance. It always works for me.

We waved Katie and Jon off on honeymoon a few hours later. My sister hugged me fiercely and told me I was the best sister ever. She doesn't have any other sisters for comparison, but I appreciated the compliment anyway.

Sometime after midnight, I went home to my apartment. It felt quiet and empty. I'd always been happy living alone, but tonight loneliness washed over me like a dark cloud. It must be the aftermath of the wedding. All that smiling and socialising had taken its toll.

I read for a while, hoping to get sleepy, but unfortunately stayed wide awake. Some time later, I looked at the clock — two in the morning. Reading was really not going to help.

I slid out of bed, and padded into the living room, dragging the duvet with me.

An old film might do it.

I channel surfed for a while. However many reality shows were there on the cable channels these days? Beautiful bodies, ugly bodies, people stranded on islands, people with tattoos inked on every inch of their bodies, and people stranded in the jungle — eating maggots. Eugh! Finally I came across a really old episode of *The Man From U.N.C.L.E.*, and was asleep in seconds.

7

Nik let himself into the house, and headed straight for his laptop. He'd enjoyed the party, quite a lot actually. He liked the Halloween theme too, albeit three weeks early — which he didn't think mattered a bit to the party-goers. He really appreciated the number of girls dressed as Cat Woman — in fact, probably the whole reason for an early Halloween party was to encourage girls to dress up as Cat Woman. His friends Jake and Dave were there, and he always enjoyed their company. They'd all known each other for a long time, so the banter was instant and easy. The whole evening had been just what he needed to cheer him up. The guys had hooted with laughter over Jemima and Nik's disastrous attempt at online dating. They still couldn't understand how he remained unattached.

'Mate, I have a great idea,' Dave had

said. 'Speed dating.'

Well this was a new one on Nik.

'As in very fast dates?' Nik had been puzzled.

They hooted with laughter again.

Then Dave explained. Nik had been quite interested. It sounded a good idea at the time.

So now Nik sat at the table with his laptop and did a search for speed dating in his area. It turned out there were two pubs locally that ran speed dating evenings. One wasn't too far from the nursery either, so he could theoretically go straight there after work.

'No need to sign up', the website said. All he had to do was pay a twenty-pound entry fee on the door. Then he could spend all evening meeting lots of different women — in fact he'd be meeting a different women every eight to ten minutes. It sounded perfect. Although he hoped Jemima didn't turn up again. That could potentially be detrimental to his health, and actually his reputation too, seeing as she thought he had a drink problem. He wondered idly whether she'd finished knitting Harry and Meghan yet.

He made sure to read the small print,theverysmallprintandthe exceptionally small print this time. The speed dating was for over twenty-ones and under thirty-fives only. Nik wasn't sure how they could make sure, but then the very small print assured him IDs would be thoroughly checked before entry was allowed. He felt reassured.

The next Speed Date Night was advertised for Wednesday at six-thirty. The nursery closed at six on Wednesdays, so providing Tom's mum managed to avoid the pitfalls of signal failures on the Jubilee Line, he'd be able to make it.

The familiar bats in his belly told him that merely the thought of the evening made him nervous. He wondered whether he could persuade Dave and Jake to join him, but then thought he wouldn't be able to cope with another disastrous date night if it included their ragging. And then if one of them should meet an amazing girl, and he *didn't*, it would make him even more nervous about ever trying again. Decisions, decisions. He'd sleep on it.

* * *

Wednesday evening, and Nik found himself in a queue outside The White Hart. He surreptitiously eyed the other participants. They looked a fairly motley crew if he was honest. Some of the men looked plain scary, and none too clean either. He thought they probably just fancied a night out, without any intention whatsoever of actually dating anyone. A few men looked a lot older than thirty-five as well. Did everyone lie about their age these days? Then he wondered how many were actually already married. Potential dating was obviously making him cynical.

Several women appeared to have arrived in giggling gaggles. *Why did girls always go around together?* No wonder they weren't with anyone, no man in his right mind would ever approach a load of girls on his own. A recipe for disaster and embarrassment if ever he saw one. Some of the girls looked attractive and friendly, which gave Nik encouragement. If they were ever separated from one another, they might even be approachable.

A dog barked incessantly from somewhere near the pub, and Nik wondered whether the poor thing was okay. Dogs didn't usually bark all the time unless something was wrong. He wondered whether to investigate, but the queue of people had started to edge closer towards the doors, and he became distracted.

The pub opened its doors to their private room at exactly six-thirty, and they all filed in. It took quite a while for the beefy-looking man on the desk to meticulously check everyone's ID, but eventually all the men who passed scrutiny were sitting behind tables, whilst the women sat at the bar sipping their free cocktails.

Nik wiped his clammy hands on his clean jeans, and smiled gratefully at the barmaid as she delivered the beer he'd ordered — bottled and cold this time. He took a large swig and glanced at the man on his left. He looked as wretched as Nik felt, so he didn't try to engage him in conversation. Definitely a computer nerd, Nik thought; pale-faced and very skinny. Probably never went outside much at all. Perhaps he combusted in strong sunlight like Dracula.

He wondered what the hell he was doing here. In fact, he wondered what any of them were doing here. Were they all so useless at communicating with the opposite sex? He suspected he was the only person in the room with a deadline, but that was a whole different issue. He sighed. He could still hear the poor dog barking too, and resolved to have a word with somebody about it before he left tonight.

Somewhere a bell sounded and Nik jumped. He looked up to see the girls all heading towards him and his fellow men. This was potentially the scariest thing he'd ever done in his life. Perhaps he could still make a run for the door?

'Hey there.' The rich American twang was unmistakeable.

Expecting Dolly Parton, Nik looked up and made eye contact with the voluptuous blonde standing in front of his table.

'Er . . . hey?'

The blonde sat down and offered her hand. Nik shook it, barely escaping getting his own hand shredded by the immaculately varnished, bright red talons.

'My name's Louanne. What's yours, hon?'

'Nik.' His voice came out like a strangled toad's. 'Where are you from?'

'From a liddle biddy place near Nashville.'

'Holidaying?'

'Sure. Doin' Europe.'

'Why are you here this evening?'

'To meet darlin' li'l cutie-pies like you.'

Nik wasn't sure whether she was serious or not, but before he could croak anything else, Louanne continued.

'Do you like country music Nik?'

The Dolly Parton vision flitted through Nik's thoughts again. 'Some of it,' he admitted. 'Do you sing?'

'Everyone living in and near Nashville sings, hon.'

'Do you know Dolly Parton?'

Louanne threw back her blonde head and laughed loudly. 'Well I know who she *is*.'

Nik grinned. 'Silly question, huh?'

'That lady has so many bodyguards, I reckon even her husband has to get an appointment to speak to her.'

At that moment a bell sounded, making them both jump.

Louanne stood up.

'Jeez, that sure was fast. Gotta go hon. Here's my cell phone and email. Give me a call sometime.' She handed Nik a small business card with bright red lips printed on one side and information on the other. 'See y'all.'

Well she was certainly different. He'd like to find out whether she could sing like Dolly. Although he wondered what his father would make of Louanne from her 'liddle biddy place near Nashville'.

A small brunette sank into the vacated seat. She couldn't have been more different to Louanne if she'd tried. She pushed her glasses further up her nose and blinked owlishly at Nik.

'Hi,' he said helpfully. 'I'm Nik.'

'Jane,' she said in a whisper.

Nik felt almost sorry for her. She appeared even more nervous than he felt.

'What do you do, Jane?'

'I'm a librarian.'

That figured.

Jane fiddled with her pearl necklace, and straightened her navy-blue cardigan a few times. She looked like an extra from a 1940s film.

She didn't ask him anything about himself, so they talked about books until the bell sounded, when she moved off with obvious relief to the guy next door. He looked much more her type, Nik thought.

Still, he was no expert. She might have been a real party animal, although he'd bet any amount of money she wasn't. But he *did* know a lot more about the indexing system in the local library than when he'd arrived.

The evening began to blur a bit after that. So many girls. Girls of all shapes and sizes. Giggly ones, quiet ones, obnoxious ones. He actually wished Louanne would come back.

The bell sounded again.

There was a general scuffle around the room, and Nik looked up to see his next introduction. This time he approved.

The girl who sank into the seat in front of him was slight, dark-haired and attractive.

'Hello, I'm Susie,' she said.

'Nik,' he replied with a smile.

'Do you like lizards, Nik?'

'Well I couldn't eat a whole one.' *Damn his stupid sense of humour.*

Susie looked utterly horrified. 'Eat?' she squeaked.

'Sorry . . . so   sorry . . . my   poor attempt at humour . . .'

'Oh.' Susie still looked horrified.

'Do you keep lizards?' Nik felt he was sinking in a quagmire, and desperately attempted to save the situation.

'Yes I have two Chinese water dragons, a bearded dragon and two geckos.'

'Sounds . . . erm . . . fun.' Actually Nik thought it sounded anything but. He wondered whether her house smelt strange.

'And six tarantulas. I just *love* spiders don't you?'

Nik had never really thought about it.

'I guess . . . ' This was going well. Not.

Saved by the bell, Nik watched Susie scurry away to scare the pants off the nerd next door, who, in turn, was looking around the room, presumably to find Jane. He'd been right — those two really were a match made in heaven.

'Ladies and Gentlemen, the next introduction will be the last for this evening.'

Thank all the heavens for that. All Nik wanted to do was go home and sink a few more beers. His attention was suddenly drawn to a kerfuffle near the door. A tall, slim, dark-haired girl appeared to be having an altercation with the truculent Mr Beefy on the door.

' . . . *not* leave a dog chained up outside like that,' he heard her say. And then, 'I'm going to report you.'

Something about the girl seemed familiar.

She opened the main door to the street, and started to stomp out, but for some reason, she glanced back into the room.

Nik felt a jolt of familiarity in his stomach as his gaze met midnight-blue eyes. His spirits soared — it was the vision from the wedding. Thank heavens for small towns. And there was no 'Mr Impossibly Handsome' in sight either. She tossed back her mane of glossy, black hair and grinned at him impishly. He grinned back like an idiot. What on earth was she talking about dogs with the security guy for? And whatever would she think seeing him here, taking part in a speed date night? With a cheery wave, she left, and the door swung closed behind her. Damn. He had half risen to his feet to go after her, when a very middle-class voice close by said, 'Hi, I'm Toyah.'

Startled, he turned to look at the person who'd spoken. Half expecting to see a red-haired punk singer from the eighties, he wasn't completely disappointed. This Toyah was clearly the daughter of true punk fans, with her thatch of carrot-coloured hair, eerily similar to her namesake, a ring through her nose and a silver bolt through her left eyebrow.

Dressed entirely in black, her bare arms sported some rather beautiful and intricate gothic tattoos.

'Nice to meet you,' he muttered.

'Have you even heard of the singer, Toyah?' The girl demanded, tilting her chair back on two legs and regarding him with suspicion.

Nik assured her he had, and went on to share his knowledge. She looked vaguely impressed. He guessed he was probably far too normal looking for a goth chick like her, but they had a fun chat about music nevertheless. They parted amicably, and even walked out together. At least it had saved him from the lizard lady. He wondered where the lovely Annie had gone. He couldn't hear the dog barking any more, and wondered whether she'd taken it upon herself to rescue it.

8

For some weird reason I woke up feeling inexplicably happy. Then I remembered why. Mr Hunky from the car park had been at the speed dating night, which meant he was single. I found it difficult to believe he needed to resort to speed dating. It's been some time since I felt interested in anyone new, but there was definitely something interesting about him.

Work takes up a lot of my time, and the local single men didn't exactly inspire me with enthusiasm on the dating front. But how lucky for me, and the poor dog at the pub, that I was on my way back from Mum's last night. For once, I was in the right place at the right time. I stopped to have a go at the man on the door about his dog. I still felt determined to report him. The poor dog was tethered by such a short chain that it couldn't even sit down, and there wasn't any food or water I could see. The man clearly wasn't even capable of looking after a slow worm. Tim, my boss, is always so good when I take similar problems like this in to work, and I felt sure he'd help this time too. My main problem now, apart from rescuing the poor dog at the pub, is obviously going to be how to meet Nik properly, preferably without knocking him over. I have no idea where he lives or where he works, or even what he does. For all I know, he could clean sewers for a living, or live in a cardboard box under the bypass — although he looked far too clean for either of those.

'His name's Nik,' I sighed down the phone to Katie. It felt as if my sister had been on honeymoon for ever. 'Are you ever coming home?'

Katie giggled. She does a lot of that these days. Crazy in love, I suppose. Lucky her.

'We've only been away a week, Annie,' she said. 'Huh.'

'We still have another whole week.'

'Uh-huh.' I could hear Jon calling her, and sighed again. 'Sure, see you when you get home.'

I tossed my mobile on the bed, and headed for the shower. Whatever the gorgeous Nik did or didn't do, I still had a job to go to.

The day whizzed by, as most days at work tend to do. An Irish wolfhound with a cut leg caused mayhem. Not surprising as he probably weighed more then me and the vet put together.

His owner was a small, bird-like woman who apologised profusely. She probably had to apologise often to a lot of people. Why do little people always go for ginormous dogs? And she called him Fluffy. *Seriously?*

'After Hagrid's three-headed dog in Harry Potter,' she puffed, as we tried to hold Fluffy still for Tim to put in a couple of stitches.

Fluffy's head was the size of a donkey's — thank goodness he only had one — and he stood higher than most donkeys.

'He's a real sweetie most of the time.'

'I'm sure.' I hung on to his collar for grim death. I didn't want him to eat my boss and he appeared to be more than capable.

After Fluffy had been stitched and given antibiotics, we watched him launch himself out of the surgery with his tiny owner on the end of the lead.

Tim, and I exchanged looks of relief.

'Who's next?' he asked.

I glanced at the computer screen. 'Erm . . . Hercules.'

He rolled his eyes. 'What's he? An elephant?'

Hercules turned out to be a hissing, spitting fluffball of a ginger kitten with sharp teeth and far too many claws. A lot easier to hold still at least, although I got scratched and bitten for my trouble. Luckily, Hercules only needed the second of his inoculations, so his visit was a fairly short one. Never a dull moment working with animals that's for sure.

I got home a little later than usual and was looking forward to a quiet evening with a glass of wine and a good book. I had literally just sat down when my phone rang. Katie. Of course it was.

'Hey Married Lady, how's it going?'

'Annie, you'll never guess . . .'

Why do people say that? Of course I'll never guess. She's on a Caribbean island with her new husband, basking in sunshine and romance, and I've just finished work.

'No . . .'

'Try.'

'Katie, I've just arrived home, I've been scratched, bitten, dragged around the surgery — '

'And that was just by Tim?' She cracked up at her own joke. I laughed too.

'Okay, go on, I'll buy it. What?'

'That gorgeous dreamboat you've been going on about . . .'

'Nik?'

'I think a mate of Jon's knows him.'

'How do you know he knows him? You haven't been asking around? Oh god . . .'

'Discreetly —'

'You wouldn't know discretion if it bit you on the —'

'Careful, or I won't tell you what I've found out.'

'It might not even *be* him, but go on . . .'

'Apparently the Nik Jon's mate knows, runs a nursery for pre-school kids.'

'Where?' I found I was having trouble getting my head around the information.

'Where what?'

Apparently so was Katie.

'Where's the nursery?'

'Oh I've got no idea, I'm on honeymoon.' I felt a bit mean then. Of course she was.

'Then I thank you, oh wise and newly married one. I'll go into Miss Marple mode and see what I can find out.'

'You're welcome. I hope you manage to find out more.'

'I'm sure I can. I'll have a look at local nurseries online. Katie, you're a doll, thanks.'

'See ya soon.'

And she was gone.

I fired up my laptop and did a quick search for pre-school nurseries in the area. Unsurprisingly, there were quite a few. After a lot of scrolling, I found *his* nursery, together with a very nice photo of the man himself. A thrill ran through me. I'd found him! Nikolaas Knoll. His name sounded Scandinavian. He looked a bit Scandinavian too, with his corn-coloured hair. I stared at the picture for a while, and then decided I really needed that glass of wine now. Drooling is so unattractive.

I had no clue what to do with the information. Borrow a child? Pretend to have a child? Turn up without a child, like some psycho who stole kids?

I sipped wine and read all about Nik's nursery. He had a fair-sized plot of land there, and according to the website, there was an area with assorted animals. Nik had a goat, some rabbits, a Shetland pony, and, somewhat randomly, a young reindeer. Were reindeer Scandinavian? I couldn't remember. I found myself looking online at reindeer. '*Reindeer are known as Caribou in North America and Canada.*' You learn something every day. Well, if any of the animals were ever ill, perhaps he'd call Tim.

Then I did have an idea. A real humdinger. I had some flyers advertising the practice and tomorrow was my day off . . .

9

Nik drifted off in a daydream. He was supposed to be going through the books, but Annie's lovely face with her midnight-blue eyes kept appearing in front of him, as she smiled her lovely smile. Actually, he'd thought of little else but Annie since the speed dating evening. Except for the disturbing dream he'd had that same night; a very lurid dream, involving lizards and tattoos. One of the lizards had a pierced chin with a large silver hoop through it, and he remembered vaguely thinking it must be illegal and very cruel to lizards, when the alarm clock woke him up.

He forced his attention back to the books. Sometimes he wondered what he paid accountants for. He did most of the work for them after all, especially with the amount of spreadsheets he put together. But at least they dealt with the tax office.

Sally, his wonderful assistant, peered around the door. 'Coffee?'

He grinned at her. 'You are an angel of mercy. Yes please.'

'Oh I just had a call from one of the local vet's surgeries asking whether you were signed up with a vet.'

'We're not, are we?'

'Not as far as I know.'

'Maybe we should be then.'

'I'll ring back and tell them to send details.'

'Thanks Sally.'

* * *

With lunchtime over and the younger children tucked up for a nap, Nik managed to email his spreadsheets to the accountants. He breathed a sigh of relief. He really needed to schedule a chat with Sally soon about Lucinda. The nice side of him thought she deserved a chance, but the tougher side didn't agree. There was *still* something about her that didn't quite ring true. He felt she wouldn't fit in too well with his other staff and she didn't strike him as a team player. Perhaps that was the problem. Sometimes mutual friends were a pain when they were trying to help their other friends. What was the saying? 'A friend in need is a pain in the . . . ?' Except he didn't know Lucinda at all, just the mutual friend, and he did feel sorry she was in need of a job — although, she didn't appear to be on the bread line in any way. She'd turned up to the interview driving a new Audi, and whilst he was definitely no expert on women's clothing, hers looked expensive to his untrained eye.

He sighed, and stood up to go and find Sally, when the lady herself knocked on the door again.

'Nik? There's someone here from the vet's to see you.'

'Did we ask them to come in?' He felt confused, a phone call *and* a visit on the same day? It seemed more than a little keen to him. Perhaps even overkill.

Sally looked a little embarrassed. 'No,

sorry, it's apparently her day off and when she rang, she offered to bring in some leaflets about the practice. I hope you don't mind?'

'No, it's fine. I'll come out.'

He felt a little miffed that the pushy vet had sent someone personally instead of emailing their details, but stopped short when he spotted the tall, slim, dark-haired girl in reception.

Surely not . . . ?

She turned as he approached, and a pair of bright midnight eyes twinkled at him. She held her hand out to him.

'Hi . . . Nik isn't it?'

What were the chances of that? He wondered whether he'd actually conjured her up. Contrary to everyone else's beliefs he really did believe in magic, but he would be keeping that piece of information secret.

'Yes, well remembered. Can I help?'

'I work for the local vet,' she began. 'I rang your manager this morning. As it's my day off, I thought I'd drop some leaflets off to you. I hope that's okay?'

She delved into a large bag and pulled a bundle of leaflets out to prove her point.

Nik glanced down. '*Ashley Wood Veterinary Practice,*' he read. '*Tim Sturgess MRCVS, 8 High Street, Ashley Wood, Herts.*'

'Are you Mrs Sturgess?'

She laughed. 'Good heavens no,' she said. 'I'm the practice nurse.'

A quick flash of relief ran through Nik at her laughing dismissal. So she wasn't attached to the good-looking guy from the wedding, and neither was she married to the local vet. Things were definitely looking up. He felt magic in the air.

'We have a few animals here. Would you like to see them?'

'I'd love to.'

Nik went over to a large set of double doors, keyed in a code on the wall panel and pushed a door open.

'Sally, I'm just popping out to the animals.'

'Okay.' A disembodied voice answered.

A wall of sound followed her voice; a

melee of excited shrieks and laughter. Nik shut the door hurriedly. 'Obviously this is no longer quiet time.'

'Obviously.'

He led her out the front door and around the side of the building.

'We have mostly small animals for the little ones to hold; rabbits and guinea pigs, but we also have a pony, a goat and a reindeer.'

'Reindeer is an odd choice for a nursery.'

'We have some on my family farm. This one doesn't get along too well with the adult reindeer, so I brought him here until he grows up a bit.'

'You have a farm with reindeer?'

Nik laughed. 'I know, it's a bit mad isn't it?'

'You don't . . . *eat* them . . . ?'

Nik shuddered, and the lizard lady flitted through his memory again. 'Absolutely not. I'm pescetarian.'

They reached the paddock and he watched Annie glance across at the young reindeer. He felt the usual tug of emotion when it raised its head and appeared to be looking straight at him with large brown eyes.

'Hey Rudy.' At the sound of his voice, the reindeer immediately started towards them.

'Wow, you've got him well trained.' Annie leaned on the gate, watching the creature come closer. 'He's not nervous of us at all.'

Nik rummaged in his jacket pocket and brought out some treats, which Rudy polished off with relish.

'Cupboard love I think,' he said with a smile.

She grinned back, and he watched the sparkle in her amazing eyes. Any kind of love with her sounded like a good idea to him.

Rudy head-butted Nik's arm in the hope of more treats, and he opened the gate just wide enough for Annie to sidle through.

'I don't think he'll escape, if he thinks there are more goodies in my pocket, but you never know.' He followed her into the field and secured the gate behind him.

He led the way across the field towards a smaller enclosure with a series of hutches. Rudy trotted behind him, occasionally giving him a hopeful nudge.

'You get more treats when we leave,' Nik told him. 'Otherwise you'll get fat.'

Annie laughed. 'Story of my life.'

Nik gave her an appraising look. 'Somehow I don't believe that.' Then he wanted to kick himself for being too personal.

After he'd shown her Gertie the goat, and Merlin, the wicked little Shetland pony (*don't turn your back on him, he likes to nip at body parts*), they went into the enclosure to look at the guinea pigs and rabbits.

Annie looked perfectly at home cuddling Rufus, the large lop-eared rabbit, but then Nik supposed she would, being a veterinary nurse.

'I don't suppose you get much call for treating large animals?' he asked as he put a squeaking guinea pig back in its hutch. Stroking Rufus goodbye, she handed him to Nik so he could put him back in his hutch too.

'Well a lot of people around here have horses,' she said. 'And we have two sheep farms on our books, so lambing is a busy time.'

'No reindeer though?'

'We will have if you register.' She grinned. 'Tim would be thrilled.'

'I never got around to registering officially with a vet,' Nik agreed. 'We've been pretty lucky so far with ailments, but better safe than sorry.'

'You can register online if you like.'

A sudden flash of the online dating website made Nik draw in a sharp breath.

'Or you can pop in anytime,' Annie continued.

'Why don't I come in tomorrow, register with the practice and take you to lunch?' Nik didn't know what had just happened. Spontaneity was not usually his thing. Very unlike him to jump in feet first, or actually jump at all.

'My lunch hour tomorrow's quite late,

two until three. Does that fit in with you?'

'Absolutely.' He'd make sure of it.

'Then you're on.'

After Annie had left, Nik sat staring at his account books, going back over the conversation they'd had. Had he come across like a dork? Too pushy? Not pushy enough? Then he consoled himself by the fact she'd said yes. She. Said. YES. She had agreed to a lunch date. Who needed online dating?

10

What do people wear on a first date? More importantly what could I wear for a lunch date? And what exactly *is* a lunch date? I still had to work after lunch and if I turned up for work in anything fancier than usual, I knew for a fact I'd never live it down — which meant Nik would probably guess I'd gone to an inordinate amount of trouble over my appearance. And that could be embarrassing for both of us.

I decided I needed to talk to Katie, my style guru. I wished she'd come home.

Luckily for me, she rang to see whether I'd found Nik's nursery, and was suitably impressed when I told her not only my genius idea, but the fact that it had worked.

'Wow, Annie, that's quite brilliant,' she said with admiration in her voice. 'He didn't think you were stalking him?'

Trust Katie to think of a downside.

'Stalking?' I spluttered. 'He's taking me to lunch, so I think probably not.'

'What are you going to wear?'

My stomach did a downward plunge. I always wore jeans and a T-shirt to work. We all wore dark blue lab coats in the surgery, so most of our clothes were covered up.

'My problem is, if I turn up to work in a little black number, and then Nik arrives to buy me lunch, the whole practice will know. I'll be rumbled.'

Katie giggled.

'Stop laughing.'

'You are funny, Annie.'

'So you keep telling me.'

'Wear your normal jeans, but wear a smarter top, so when you're in the pub you won't look like a stable hand.'

I felt affronted. 'Is that what you think I look like?'

'No of course not, but you aren't exactly in the glossy *Vogue* stakes at work, are you?'

I sighed. 'I suppose not.'

Katie did a quick virtual run-through of my wardrobe, which didn't take too long, and we agreed on my grey and black striped sweater, which is light enough to wear underneath my lab coat without me suffering from heat exhaustion, and warm enough to wear under my leather jacket in chilly mid-October without dying from frostbite. The weather had certainly turned autumnal this week.

I was under strict instructions to check my jeans were clean and free from paw prints, dog hair and dribble, and if they weren't, to wash them and get them dry overnight.

'Thanks Katie.'

'Good luck. He'd better be worth it, or *I* will hunt *him* down!'

I laughed. 'Thanks.'

'Love you loads.'

'Back at you.' I went off to check my jeans for dribble and dog hair.

★   ★   ★

For once, the morning dragged at work. Usually we were so busy and time flew by, but today we'd only had two cats for their annual injections, which were dealt with very quickly.

I glanced up from reading the paper to find Tim looking at me.

'What?' I asked, warily.

'Are you wearing make-up?'

Damn. If we'd been busy as normal, he'd never have noticed. In fact if we'd been busy, I could be wearing a black bin-liner and he wouldn't have noticed.

I gave him a warning glare. 'Don't say a word.'

He looked like he wanted to say more, but mimed zipping his mouth shut instead. If he said anything to Nik, I thought I might die of embarrassment.

Nik arrived at exactly two, his friendly grin charming our receptionist into a melted puddle. I watched him register with the practice through the little window in the surgery door, and then decided to go out and claim him before she got any ideas.

'Going for lunch,' I told Tim, who looked as if he might explode. 'Say nothing — Hi Nik,' I said brightly. 'All signed up?'

'Yes. Ready for lunch?' His glance told me I was still wearing my lab coat.

'I'll get my jacket.'

I went back into the surgery and nearly ran into Tim who had been watching through the window.

'New client,' I said. 'Smarties Nursery in Church Road, three guinea pigs, two rabbits, one goat, one Shetland and a reindeer.'

'Reindeer?' said Tim faintly. 'Did you say reindeer?'

'Yep.' I took off my lab coat and hung it on a peg behind the door, pulling on my leather jacket. 'A reindeer, just perfect for Christmas.'

'I expect we'll be eating turkey for lunch this Christmas as usual.'

'Ha ha. See you later.'

'Have a nice lunch.'

I turned back at the door but Tim looked innocent. Too innocent. I gave him a stern look, and closed the door firmly behind me.

'See you later, Jen,' I said to the receptionist, who was still ogling Nik. Well who could blame her? Actually I might at a later date, but for now I'd let her off.

We walked up the high street and Nik suggested The Wheatsheaf for lunch, so we crossed over the road, and went in to the main bar.

The Wheatsheaf is Ashley's only gastro pub, having been taken over by a minor celebrity chef two years ago. Hardly the cheapest of lunch venues either, but I wasn't going to argue. It felt warm and cosy in the bar, thanks to the welcoming log fire burning in the large inglenook. We found a table in a corner near the fire, and after a quick look at the menu, Nik went up to the bar to order our food and drinks.

Real food at lunch time — what a treat. I usually only managed a quick sandwich between patients when we're busy, which sounds weirder than it's meant to. I had a sudden mental picture of being trapped between Fluffy and another large dog whilst trying to eat a sandwich. My lurid imagination again . . .

Nik came back with our drinks and sat down.

'Do you come here often?' he asked with a grin.

'Hardly ever,' I said. 'Especially at the moment, after my sister's wedding.'

'Surely you didn't have to help pay for the wedding?'

'No, thank goodness. But my dress cost . . . a lot . . .'

'From what I remember, it looked worth every penny.'

'Thanks.' Hearing Nik say that, certainly made the dress worth every penny, and more. I sipped at my lime and soda, wishing it was a large glass of red wine to stop me feeling like a nervous schoolgirl. But we have a strict no alcohol rule at work, which is fair, because we sometimes have lives at stake.

'So you don't drink alcohol?'

'Not during a work day,' I said, wondering if he'd managed to read my thoughts. 'Too many important patients to look after.'

'Ah.'

I gave his beer a pointed look.

'It's my afternoon off.'

'Lucky.'

Our food arrived then, and looked every bit as amazing as I'd expected. Gourmet fish pie, with prawns and scallops, for both of us. I remembered Nik saying he was pescetarian, so I'd played safe and ordered the same.

'This looks incredible,' I said.

We ate in silence for . . . actually not that long at all. The food was delicious and the conversation flowed. We found we liked the same kind of films, and we shared a similar sense of humour. We laughed a lot and I felt we'd known each other for ages rather than just two days.

I decided I liked looking at him too, especially as the glow from the fire illuminated his corn-coloured hair and made his grey eyes glint with humour. I'm normally not given to poetic rubbish, but something about Nik made me feel different, softer than my usual practical self.

Reluctantly at five to three, I said I had to go back to work. Nik walked back with me.

'How about a proper drink later?' he asked, as I paused at the surgery door.

'I'd like that.'

We arranged to meet in The White Hart at eight, and I couldn't resist a quip about being thankful he hadn't been successful at speed dating. Nik gave a rueful grin, and said that evening had put him off lizards for life. When I looked puzzled, he promised to fill me in later.

11

Nik popped back to work to feed the animals and bed them down for the night. Even on his afternoon off, he liked to check on the animals himself. Rudy looked pleased to see him, and followed him round the paddock as he filled the water trough and hay nets.

'If you hadn't been such a stroppy git you could be back on the farm with all the others,' Nik told him, fondling Rudy's velvety ears.

Large brown eyes stared back.

'You should know your old man is in charge.'

Rudy snorted.

'A lesson for you too,' said a voice behind him.

Nik jumped and spun around. An extremely short man with a face like a seasoned walnut, looked up at him with eyes the colour of a winter sea.

'Bloody hell, Harry! What are you doing here? Apart from giving me heart failure, that is.'

'I needed to see you,' the little man replied, picking stray bits of hay from Rudy's coat.

'About?'

'The family business.' Harry looked behind him, and seeing no one there, he continued. 'Your father is concerned about you.'

'Why?'

'You know why.'

'There's time . . .'

'We'll be in November soon enough.'

'If I rush things, I may scare her off.'

Harry looked interested. 'So there is someone?'

'I hope so.'

'Good. That's really very good. Can I tell your father?'

'Not yet. I'll tell him as soon as I can, I promise.'

'He worries.'

'I know.' Nik turned back to Rudy, stroking his glossy neck. 'But I need to take things slowly, and I have to be sure . . .'

He was talking to no one but the reindeer. The paddock behind him was empty again.

* * *

Nik arrived at The White Hart at seven-fifteen. He always hated to be late, and tended to over-compensate. Although now he started to worry he'd arrived ridiculously early. If Annie didn't turn up, he would look even more of an idiot — and for longer. Luckily, he needn't have worried; she breezed in at five to eight looking fabulous, and he grinned at her like a love-struck idiot.

'What can I get you?' He started to stand up, but she waved him back down.

'I'll get it. What would you like?'

He looked at his empty bottle, and turned it round so she could see the label.

She darted off towards the bar, and then he started worrying she'd think he either drank too much too fast — or he'd been here for ages. Either way it didn't look good. Perhaps she wouldn't over-think anything. Not like he did anyway.

Annie returned with two bottles of beer and put one in front of Nik with a flourish.

'How was your afternoon off?'

'Well I still had to go back to feed the animals,' he said, taking a swig from his bottle. 'How was your afternoon?'

Annie went on to tell him about the client who'd come in with a small cardboard box containing a tiny baby hedgehog she'd found in her garden.

'It must have been very young, its spines were still soft,' said Annie. 'Tim went round to the woman's house after surgery to see whether he could find the mother.'

'What if he doesn't?'

'He'll take the baby to the wildlife sanctuary in Brackenhurst.'

'Will it survive?'

'It should do. They're amazing there.'

'The NHS could learn a lot from you guys.'

'Put people in cardboard boxes?'

'Isn't there a song about that?'

His phone rang. His father, naturally. Apologising to Annie, he answered the call.

'Dad. How are you?'

'Harry says he came to see you.'

'He did.'

'And you have something to tell me?'

'Now's not a good time, Dad. I'm out with someone.'

'A girl?'

'Dad . . .' Nik felt his cheeks flush and hoped Annie didn't notice.

'Please call me later.'

The phone went dead, and Nik stuffed it back in his jacket pocket. Annie was watching him curiously.

'Everything okay?'

'My Dad rings me . . . a lot.' Nik gave an apologetic shrug. 'I don't get back to him as often as I should. Work and stuff.'

'If you're worried about leaving the animals, I can always look after them for you. No charge. Well maybe a lunch or two.' She grinned.

And Nik fell just a little bit in love at that moment.

12

I kept going over the evening with Nik in my head. Offering to look after his animals could have appeared too pushy, and I felt worried, so I went over the conversation again and again. He didn't appear to mind me offering. At least I don't think he did. Sometimes I get nervous and I babble, and then all sorts of things blurt out.

I felt consoled by the fact he'd asked to see me at the weekend, Saturday evening in fact, in The Wheatsheaf. It's a very couply place on a Saturday, apparently. Perhaps Nik doesn't know that. I've never actually been in there on a Saturday, which says everything about my social life.

How I wished Katie was home. She's always so good with clothes advice and even better at keeping me calm. It's obvious now how she managed to get married first. I'm a gibbering idiot who's always in scruffy jeans and wellies, as well as often being covered in animal hair and drool. I took solace in the fact that Nik obviously likes animals too. Rudy the reindeer certainly likes him — not too sure about Merlin, but then I don't think he likes anyone much.

Friday evening saw me close to blind panic. A huge tom had thrown up a massive furball over my lab coat, and my best jeans. You may ask why I was wearing my best jeans to work, and all I can say, is that my work jeans had suffered an even worse fate the day before. The joys of working with nervous animals . . .

I had two options: wash the jeans and hope they dried — minus furball stains — by early Saturday evening, or go into town in my decidedly scruffy (but clean) work jeans after work on Saturday morning, to buy something new. The buying something new would be favourite if I was Katie. She can go in to any chain store, any designer store or even any market stall, and whatever she buys will look fabulous. The huge plus, of being blonde and gorgeous, with a perfectly proportioned body. Not that I'm bitter or anything . . . she's . . . well she's Katie.

I sat morosely in front of the television, not really noticing the programme, and glugging from a bottle of beer. Needs must.

Katie rang like she always does when I need her the most. She really is amazing, and possibly psychic.

'I was just thinking about you,' I said.

'Snap.'

'You must be coming home soon . . . ?'

'We're back sometime tomorrow.'

'Thank all the gods in every heaven in the universe.'

'Awww, Annie, have you missed me?'

'I need help and you're the only person in the world who can help me,' I wailed just a little bit plaintively. I began to explain.

'Just go into town after work and buy a nice smart pair of black trousers.'

'Black trousers?'

'Yes. He's seen you in jeans — knowing

you — several times, so now's the time to ramp up your look a bit. I think I'm coming home just in time.'

'In time for what?'

'To stop you from blowing it.'

'But I don't have anything to go with black trousers . . .'

Katie made a rude noise down the phone. 'You dingbat.' She used my favourite insult and made me laugh. 'Every colour goes with black. Even more black. You should know that more than anyone else on the planet.'

'Okay . . . and of course I do. I'm just a bit nervous.'

'If you want my advice, and you do need it, I think you should buy a top in sizzling red to go with the black trousers. With your hair, you'll look sensational.'

'Not like Mata Hari?'

'Hari . . . *who?*'

'Never mind.'

'Trust me, he won't be able to take his eyes off you.'

'He won't be blinded by all the sizzling red?'

'He'll be besotted.'

'Thanks Katie.'

She blew a kiss down the phone this time, and promised she'd see me soon. Strangely, I couldn't wait to have her back. If anyone asked me, I would have sworn she'd been on honeymoon for at least a month. Even two months. Not that I'd been counting the days or anything, but we seemed to be veering towards November at a rate of knots, and I felt as though I'd been sister-less for a very long time. Annoying little sister she may be, but I really wanted her home.

13

For only the second time in my recent clothes shopping life, I'd been successful. Katie would be so proud of me, and if the truth be known, I did feel kind of smug. I'd been in to town, scoured the local branch of John Lewis, and emerged some time later, with a pair of very flattering skinny black jeans, and a gorgeous scarlet silk top with tiny black rose buds all over it. Yes I know Katie had said to buy trousers, but I look better in jeans, and they fitted like a glove. They'd cost a small fortune, but hey, who's counting? That's what credit cards are for.

Back at the flat, I hung up my new clothes on the outside of the wardrobe door so I could admire them for the two hours left until I put them on again. I touched the soft silk of the top. I would never have even contemplated buying anything like this normally. Katie should probably be stylist to the stars or something fabulous. She'd be good at that.

Half an hour before I needed to leave, I was doing a twirl for the umpteenth time in front of the mirror in my new finery, when Katie rang to say they were home. Jet-lagged, but home. She wanted to know where I was meeting Nik, and when I told her, she sounded incredulous.

'He's taking you to The Wheatsheaf on only the third date, on a Saturday night?'

'Katie, he probably has no idea it's a couple-fest on a Saturday.'

'Well apparently he's not exactly new in town,' she said thoughtfully, and I wondered exactly how much digging she'd been doing.

'How come I've never met him before then?'

'He's been a bit of a hermit, apparently. All work, no play kind of a person.'

That didn't sound much like Nik.

'How does Dave know him?'

'His sister's two-year-old daughter goes to his nursery, and he always picks her up on Wednesdays.'

Ah. Small town.

'Get some rest, Katie. We'll catch up tomorrow at Mum and Dad's.'

'Actually, I'll see you in a minute.'

My doorbell rang. Did I mention my sister is quite mad?

I went to let her in, and she wafted into the living room looking sleeker, blonder and more tanned. She gave an approving whistle when she saw me.

'Perfect, Annie. Absolutely perfect. He'll probably propose.'

'I hope not.' I felt horrified. That really would send me running for the hills. 'Don't look so frightened.' Katie laughed. 'It was a joke.'

'I'd like to build up to a serious relationship over, shall we say, five years or so first?'

'Whatever you say.' Katie rummaged around in her bag and offered me a prettily wrapped package. 'I hoped you'd go with the red theme, and thought you might like this.'

I tore off the paper and revealed a candy-striped box inside. I took off the lid and gasped at the silver bangle studded with red stones.

'It's absolutely gorgeous.' I slipped it on my wrist straight away. However had Katie found a bangle with stones the colour of my new top when she hadn't even seen it? Like I said — psychic.

'I saw it at the airport on the way home, so lucky you, you get two presents from the Caribbean.'

I hugged her. 'You are totally amazing.'

'And I have to go, Jon's waiting outside. Can we drop you at The Wheatsheaf?'

'Actually, yes you can . . . wait a minute . . . ' I eyed her suspiciously. 'That doesn't mean you're going to crash my date does it?'

She gave me mock horror eyes. 'As if.'

I didn't feel too convinced, but if I didn't take the lift, I'd be late, so I pulled on my leather jacket and followed her out.

'You look like a rock chick,' she said as we went out towards their car.

I could live with that.

14

The Wheatsheaf was buzzing. Saturday night certainly seemed to be happening in this place. Nik felt relieved he'd booked a table, but worried that everyone else was part of couple, and he, of course, was early. Again. And sitting on his own. Several people glanced his way as though he should not have had the temerity to book a table for one on a Saturday night.

Relief flooded him when he saw Annie come in. Although to be fair, she would have been difficult to miss in the knockout red top she was wearing. She waved, and started to weave her way through the crowd towards him. It was then he noticed she was being followed by the Disney princess from the wedding, who in turn was being followed by the Disney prince from the wedding.

'My sister Katie wanted to meet you,'

Annie said apologetically by way of a greeting.

'I've heard a lot about you,' said Nik holding out his hand.

'None of it good I bet,' said Katie with a smile, shaking his hand.

'All of it good, I promise.' He turned to Jon. 'I'm Nik.'

'Jon.'

The two men shook hands.

'Can I get you all a drink?' Nik looked from one to the other.

Annie gave Katie raised eyebrows and then said quickly, 'They've only just got back from honeymoon and are suffering a bit with jet lag. So . . . I'll see you two tomorrow?'

Katie gave Annie a hug and whispered something that made her flush. Then she turned back to Nik. 'It was lovely to meet you,' she said. 'We should all meet up properly soon.'

'Look forward to it.'

With a cheeky grin, Katie linked her arm through Jon's and winked at Annie as they turned to make for the door.

Nik watched them leave, as Annie draped her jacket on the back of a chair before sitting down. She still looked a little flushed and he decided he'd go to her rescue. He poured a glass of wine from the bottle he'd ordered and handed it to her.

'You look gorgeous,' he said. 'So your sister's the nosey type is she?'

The tension broke and Annie laughed. 'For a younger sister, she's a bit protective.'

'Probably because we met each other while she was away.'

Annie looked impressed.

'Jon knows your friend Dave.'

'Of course he does. Everybody in town knows Dave.'

'Except me . . .'

'You don't know Dave?'

'Is that a bad thing?'

'No, it's very good for me. He really likes women with dark hair and blue eyes. Actually he really likes women. So I'm keeping you secret for a while.'

'Fine by me.'

The evening flew by and they were discussing desserts, when Nik had a strange feeling of being watched. He looked around and spotted a small man perched on a stool at the bar. Not again. *Harry.* The man had turned into a stalker. Harry raised his glass in his direction and Nik turned hurriedly back to Annie without acknowledging him, in case she noticed.

'Pavlova is quite low fat,' she was saying. 'Apart from the great dollop of cream in the middle, oh — and it comes with ice cream.'

'You don't need to watch your weight,' Nik said gallantly.

'Have you met my perfect sister?'

'Briefly.'

'Then you know why I sometimes have to watch my weight.'

Nik raised his eyebrows. In his humble opinion Annie was perfect. He was about to tell her just that, when a waitress came to the table and asked for their dessert choices. He opted for the rhubarb crumble, whilst Annie took a deep breath and ordered fresh fruit salad without cream.

'Your sister's been back in town for . . . what? An hour or so? And you're already feeling guilty about eating.'

'I ate a huge main course . . . ' She sounded defensive.

'Of caesar salad,' he reminded her. He reached across the table and took hold of her hand. He glanced down at the gleaming bangle, and turned it around on her wrist with the thumb and forefinger of his other hand. 'Like I said, you look gorgeous — you *are* gorgeous . . . and this is a lovely bracelet?'

'Wow, you really are observant.' She smiled. 'Most men wouldn't notice jewellery at all. Katie brought it back for me, she said it would go with this top.'

'And she knew you were wearing it tonight?'

'You are too clever by half.'

'Let's just stay with observant.'

When they reached the cappuccino stage, Nik risked a glance towards the bar. In true Harry fashion, he'd disappeared again, and Nik sighed with relief. He really would have to speak to his father about Harry popping up all the time. He did understand the urgency, but their constant vigilance would not help.

Annie and Nik left The Wheatsheaf at closing time and walked hand in hand towards the taxi place on the corner. They got into the same cab and Annie gave her address to the driver.

'We're all going to Mum and Dad's for lunch tomorrow,' she said suddenly, as the cab pulled out onto the main road. 'You're welcome to come, if you think you can stand the whole family in one go.'

'Count me in,' he said. 'I'll go anywhere for food.'

'Me too,' she nodded. 'Except Katie will be keeping an eagle eye on how many roasties I eat.'

'We'll take her on together,' he promised, leaning forward to kiss her gently on the lips.

15

I woke up at some ungodly hour on Sunday morning, and remembered about Nik being pescatarian. Being a kind and considerate daughter, I waited until almost seven before ringing Mum.

'What's wrong?' Mum always thinks something is wrong. But I suppose getting a call from your eldest daughter before midday on a Sunday might set alarm bells ringing.

'Nik's pescatarian.'

'Who's what, dear?'

Then I remembered she didn't know about Nik yet. If Katie hadn't been away, the whole town would know about Nik, including our parents.

'Nik is the man I've been seeing for the last week or so, and I kind of invited him to lunch today, but then I remembered you haven't met him yet, and you don't know he's pescatarian.'

There was a silence.

'Mum?'

'I'm still here, dear, just digesting the information.'

'Will that be all right?'

Another silence.

'*Mum!*'

'Sssh dear, I'm thinking of something fishy that will be complemented by roast potatoes and the vegetables I have in mind.'

My mother is quite brilliant. Never phased by anything. I remained quiet for a few minutes, then she came back on.

'I can grill a salmon steak quite quickly,' she said. 'That will work with everything else we're having. Will that be all right?'

'I love you.'

'Of course you do.'

'See you about twelve?'

'Perfect. I shall look forward to meeting this young man of yours.'

'I'm not sure he's exactly mine. Early days.'

'Has Katie met him?'

'Briefly, last night. She couldn't resist popping in to The Wheatsheaf for a look at him.'

Mum laughed. 'That's our Katie,' she said. 'She only had your best interests at heart of course.'

'Naturally.' If my tone was any drier, I'd need to be rehydrated.

I was so relieved to have sorted lunch for Nik that I fell asleep again and didn't wake up again until ten-thirty. Then of course I had my usual crisis of confidence regarding clothes. There was a very good chance, we'd take the dogs for a walk after lunch, so I decided on my blue jeans — now free from furball residue — a simple black sweatshirt and suede boots. I'd take my wellies too. There. Sorted.

I decided to text Nik and let him know there might be muddy walking later. He was picking me up at eleven-thirty, but I reasoned that anyone who keeps animals should own a pair of wellington boots.

His reply assured me he kept his boots in the car, and would definitely be up for a muddy walk with the dogs. He could just be the perfect man . . .

Checking on the animals on Sunday mornings was usually a pleasure for Nik. He loved the solitude of the field, and if he was honest, he simply loved spending time with the animals. No pressure there, other than them wanting more food — and the difficulty of keeping his body parts well away from Merlin. Aptly nick-named 'that pony', he appeared to be everywhere at the same time, nostrils flared and teeth bared.

Unfortunately for Nik, on this particular Sunday, a small, annoying visitor was perched on the five-bar gate waiting for him. Nik felt a surge of annoyance.

'What is it now Harry?'

'I'm just checking in with you.'

'You saw me last night. In fact, you saw me with Annie last night. Surely that's enough to keep you off my back for a while?'

'Your father is anxious.'

'And you're seriously pissing me off.'

'We are getting close to November

now.'

'What are you, a speaking calendar? Actually I'm sure they'd be very marketable . . . '

'Sir . . . '

Nik stopped his rant. Harry never called him sir. He only ever called his father sir. He exhaled slowly, forcing himself to calm down. He raised his eyebrows at Harry, and made a 'carry on' gesture with his hands.

'If you would just go and visit your father soon, I'm sure we could all relax a little. But time is getting on.'

'I have a business to run here, animals to look after, a new nursery assistant who I'm really not sure about and a brand new relationship that I'd very much like to spend a lot of time cultivating.'

'Believe me, we would all like you to nurture your new relationship.'

Nik opened the gate with Harry still perched on it, walked into the field, and then swung the gate closed again with a forcible bang, causing the man to jump down before he fell off.

'I have animals to feed,' he said again, striding towards the small shed where he kept the hay and other feed. Rudy, ever the optimist, followed him closely, nudging his jacket pocket every few minutes. 'And I have a lunch date which I need to change clothes for.'

'With the family.' It was a statement and Nik turned back to look at the small man.

'How do you know that?'

Harry shrugged. 'We know most things.'

Nik frowned, patting Rudy absent-mindedly. 'Look I'll pop back and see Dad next week for a couple of days, but I have to get the kids' Christmas show ready for the beginning of December, if I'm to come back the same time as usual.'

Harry nodded. 'That will have to do.'

Nik went to snap back a retort but Harry had gone again.

'Gets more like The Wizard of Oz here every day,' he murmured instead.

He fed the animals, muttering to himself all the time. His life always did get complicated at this time of year.

16

Nik parked outside Annie's address. Her flat was on the first floor of a Victorian town house. She'd told him it had belonged to her grandmother. The outside looked well cared for. The tiny square front garden had a neat privet hedge along the front, and the short concrete path led up to a black and white tiled porch. There was an entry phone on the wall by the door, with names by the buzzers. He pressed the bell for the first floor flat, even though the name by it said H. A. Berry. He wondered if H. A. Berry had been the grandmother.

A crackling from the entry phone made him jump.

'Hi?' Annie's voice sounded tinny and distorted through the speaker.

'Hey, it's Nik.'

'Come on up.'

Another buzz sounded, presumably

meaning the front door was open, so Nik pushed it and stepped inside.

Annie leaned over the bannister at the top of the stairs. 'I'm not quite ready. Come up and have a cup of coffee.'

Nik ran up the stairs, and planted a kiss on Annie's cheek. 'You look ready to me.'

'If I don't put some lippy on, my mum will think I'm ill.'

'Ah mum logic.'

'Exactly.'

He followed her in to the tiny hallway and along a passage to the kitchen. She'd already made coffee in a cafetiere, which she poured it into two mugs, then added milk to both.

'So who's H.A. Berry?' he asked suddenly.

Annie looked slightly shocked, and her cheeks flushed a pretty pink colour. 'Erm . . . actually it's me.'

'Ah, so you really are leading a double life, and you are actually a beautiful Russian spy called Helena Anouska Berryosokova. I *knew* it.'

Annie laughed. 'Idiot.'

Nik wiggled his eyebrows at her. 'You will, I think, tell me everything.' 'It's not as exciting as your idea. My name is Holly Anne Berry. I got sick of stupid Christmas jokes about my name, which — believe me — get worse the closer Christmas gets.'

Nik moved closer, and gently tucked a wayward strand of dark hair behind her ear. He kissed her gently on the lips. 'So you use your middle name.' He kissed her again. 'And you lost the holly part.' He kissed her for longer, enjoying her soft mouth responding to his.

'Mmmm.'

He wasn't sure whether that was a response to the questions or the kisses, so he drew away to see her face. She looked a little flushed but she was smiling.

'You've found me out.'

'I like the name Holly.' Actually Nik thought his family would absolutely adore the name.

'But put it with Berry?'

'I see your point.'

'Coffee,' she said.

Reluctantly he released her. 'Then apparently . . . lippy.' He grinned.

'Mum is grilling a salmon steak for you. I hope that's okay?'

'Sounds great.' He drank some coffee and allowed himself to look at Annie some more. 'You really looked a million dollars last night,' he said, and she looked pleased. 'But today I'm raising the stakes, because you've dressed for a family lunch followed by dog-walking, which is no mean feat, and you look a *gazillion* dollars.'

'Wait until you see Katie.'

He frowned. 'I don't care what Katie is wearing, and neither should you.'

'Old habits . . . ' she sighed.

He noticed she still wore the bangle Katie brought back from honeymoon for her, and wondered how long Annie had thought she was the less attractive sister. He intended to fix those thoughts once and for all. But for now, he needed to change the subject.

'Annie, your offer to look after the animals for a couple of days . . . ?'

'Sure, whenever you want.'

'I do need to go and see my parents next week. I was thinking Tuesday and Wednesday?'

'No problem.'

'Will you be able to feed them morning and evening?'

'Well, in between my clandestine dates with a world-famous actor and work, I'm sure I can squeeze them in.'

Nik laughed. 'I'm sure if anyone can charm the socks off an internationally-famous actor you can.'

'Thanks, I think.'

She darted out of the room miming putting on lipstick, and came back seconds later, with her jacket on. 'Did you bring wellington boots?'

'Absolutely. I'm good to squelch.'

'Then let's go.'

17

Lunch went well. Nik produced flowers and a bottle of wine from the back seat of his car and the parents were thrilled.

My family are always noisy, but give them a glass of wine or two, and they get a lot more noisy. Nik didn't seem phased by them at all, which earned him a lot of brownie points as far as I was concerned.

Mum did us proud as always. She obviously still thinks neither of us eat properly unless we're at the parental home. Not true. Katie eats like a horse, but remains annoyingly sylph-like, and I eat like a horse, but then have to exercise like mad afterwards. My metabolism must be asleep half the time, but thank heavens I'm a dance fanatic. I totally love whoever invented Zumba, although I really wish I'd thought of it first.

Nik and I took the family labs out — Katie and Jon having visibly shuddered at the thought of trudging through muddy fields with exuberant dogs, as opposed to watching a film on Netflix.

We arrived back at the house an hour and a half later with two very soggy dogs.

'Do you want me to hose these mangy mutts down?' I called through the kitchen window. 'Oh — ewww — Spike, get *down*.'

'Spike?' Nik raised his eyebrows.

'Yep, Spike and Dru. What can I say? We're all *Buffy* fans.'

Dru wagged her tail madly, at the sound of her name, and looked as if she was going to jump up too.

'No,' I said firmly. 'Sit.'

She sat down, pink tongue lolling out the side of her mouth.

Mum came to the kitchen window and looked out at the dogs. She made a face.

'The tin bath is in the shed,' she said. I'll get some bowls of warm water to fill it.'

Cleaning muddy dogs in a bath is always entertaining, and by the time we'd got them mud-free and dry, Nik and I weren't looking too good ourselves. Katie deigned to come out and laugh at us.

'It's okay Katie, we don't need any help,' I said, opening the back door to let the dogs in.

'Maybe you should hose each other down now?'

'And maybe I should turn the hose on you, just for fun . . . ?'

'Is this a sister thing?' Nik moved the hose out of harm's way. 'Because I should probably go inside and leave you to it.'

Just in time, Mum reappeared at the kitchen window. 'Both of you — behave yourselves, I swear you haven't changed since you were ten.'

'And I would only have been seven,' said Katie at once.

'See what I mean?' Mum said to Nik. 'Leave your boots outside, and come in for tea.'

The thought of any more food and drink made me feel a little faint, even after a long walk, but I obediently tugged off my wellies, and put my suede boots back on.

Nik looked dumbfounded when he saw the dining table groaning under the weight of scones, assorted cupcakes and a huge chocolate sponge.

'Who else is coming?' he asked.

'Even if we invited the whole street, there'd still be some left over,' I said with a grin. 'If I hadn't moved out when I did, I would have grown too huge to ever get out.'

The banter continued as I nibbled on a slice of chocolate cake, whilst Katie, Jon and Nik wolfed down most of the rest. Mum looked pleased that they were eating her and Dad out of house and home. I caught Nik watching me a couple of times and wondered why he looked so thoughtful.

'What's it like being back at work, Married Lady?' I asked Katie.

'It's all right I suppose,' she said with a shrug. 'At least Christmas is coming.'

'We're not even in November yet,' I

reminded her.

'There's a 'ber' in the month,' she said. 'And we work several months in advance.'

'Confusing,' I muttered.

'So what does your family do for Christmas, Nik?' She turned to him. I could have cheerfully throttled her. It seemed a very personal question to me.

'My family usually work right up to Christmas,' he said. 'They often don't stop until Christmas Day really. Family business.'

'What business are they in?'

Questions I hadn't even asked Nik yet myself.

'It's a toy business,' he said. 'So Christmas is our busiest time.'

That would explain him going back to help them. I decided to change the subject.

'Do you do a Christmas show at the nursery?

'Yes always, it's just the normal nativity play,' he replied. 'Only this year, we have evil Christmas trees, elves and a rampant dragon.'

'Very traditional.'

'It's a good way of getting all the kids involved because the dragon has a lot of legs.'

'I thought dragons had four legs?' Katie looked puzzled.

'How many dragons do you know?' I asked her. 'There are lots of different kinds.'

Dad raised his eyebrows at me.

'Just saying . . . '

There then followed a very surreal conversation about dragons and their legs, which had Mum and Dad roaring with laughter.

'You should drag Annie in to help with the show,' said Katie innocently. 'She's always been really good at art, and she'd be a whizz at painting scenery.'

'Now that is a very good idea.'

Actually a merciful death would probably be too quick for Katie, the way I felt about her at the moment. She smiled at me sweetly. Death by mosquito bites sounded much more appropriate. I wondered whether there were any mosquitoes still around in October.

She has this uncanny knack of asking the questions I'm thinking, then makes offers on my behalf. Is it another sister thing or is it just her? And to think I really missed her when she was on honeymoon.

18

The fat little Shetland pony and I stared at each other across the frosty paddock. He flattened his ears and showed me the whites of his eyes.

'You really don't want to mess with me, Merlin,' I told him. 'I'm a nurse.'

Clearly he didn't find me in any way scary, because he stood his ground on tiny little hooves and bared his teeth.

'Nice,' I continued. 'But I'm in charge of the munchies for a couple of days, and although you don't actually appear in need of any more food, you might want to think about it.'

Merlin snickered. It might have been a laugh, but who could tell?

Rudy butted me softly on the arm, and I stroked his neck.

'See?' I said. 'This is how to make friends and get food.'

Merlin continued to look unimpressed.

I shrugged. 'Please yourself.'

Walking over to the shed where Nik kept the feed, I unlocked the padlock with a key from the bunch he'd given me.

'And who *precisely* might you be?'

The cut-glass tones verged on strident, and came from the direction of the gate.

I turned around to see a vision from *Vogue* standing there, immaculate in skinny jeans, designer top and the sort of shoes that would never fare well in a soggy field. Her shining blonde hair was swept up in the kind of deceptively casual top-knot which takes hours to perfect. I know. I've tried.

'Annie Berry, veterinary nurse, and part-time carer for these guys,' I replied briskly.

'On whose authority?'

'The owner's.' I held up the bunch of keys. 'Which is how I come to have these. So. Who, precisely, are *you*?'

Vogue Vision glared. 'I'm Lucinda Finchley-Perry, and I work here.' I smiled sweetly. If her glare became any frostier, the water in the trough would freeze over.

'Can I help you with anything? Do you need a rabbit or something?' I struggled to keep a straight face. Lucinda didn't strike me as the rabbit-holding type.

She looked down her aristocratic nose at me. 'Just make sure everything is secure before you leave.'

'Yes Ma'am.' I couldn't resist.

I watched her picking her way carefully across the grass, and tottering back towards the nursery. Whatever could Nik have been thinking when he employed Little Ms Hoity-Toity? Oh yeah, he's a *guy*, and the Lucindas of the world change tack when a guy's around. Especially one who's the boss and looks as good as Nik. I wondered what she actually did at the nursery, I felt pretty sure I hadn't seen her the first time I visited. She didn't appear to be the nurturing, child-caring kind either, unlike Nik's lovely deputy, Sally. Perhaps she was a new addition to the staff.

Narrowing my eyes, I watched her open the main door and go inside. She

119

didn't look back at me, but then I didn't exactly look like a threat at the moment.

I was brought back to the moment by a sharp nip on my arm.

'Merlin, that is *so* not the way to make friends and get food.'

He snorted. And if I was honest, it was probably exactly the way to get food. As in, 'Feed me or lose your body parts'. I would bet any money the toddlers were allowed to feed Merlin treats which is the quickest way to make a pony snappy, in my experience. Not really his fault then.

Speaking softly, I moved closer to him, and he eyed me with deep suspicion. 'Why don't you and I have a little chat?'

He snorted again and wheeled round to gallop off, kicking up his heels as he went.

'Or not . . . ' Oh well, the gallop would do him good.

I fed the small animals first, and checked their water and bedding. The moment I started putting out the feed for Gertie and Rudy, they came straight away, whilst Merlin kept his distance. I put his food out, and fended off Gertie and Rudy, who obviously thought it was a bonus feed for them.

Merlin edged closer. His love for food would lure him eventually.

'Come on sweetie,' I said softly. 'Come and have breakfast.'

He sidled closer, still keeping a wary eye on me. I talked to him all the time, and his ears flicked back and forth, as he reached the manger. At last he started eating his food, and even allowed me to stroke him without pausing to bite or kick me. Progress.

★   ★   ★

The evening feed took longer, as I was trying to do everything by the light from the torch on my phone, with the three large animals vying for position and attention. Merlin had now decided I was his new best friend, and had taken to flattening his ears and baring his teeth at Gertie and Rudy instead of me.

'Merlin, you really do have some serious behaviour problems.' He snickered

121

softly back. It could have meant any-thing from, 'get lost' to, 'will you marry me?' but it was an improvement on the biting.

'You really do have a lovely way with animals,' a voice said behind me, and I yelped and dropped the hay I was hold-ing.

I swung around, shining the phone's torch back and forth but saw nobody.

'Who's there?'

'Sorry,' said the voice. 'I didn't mean to frighten you.'

The voice came from below my eye level, so I shone the torch downwards. Then I very nearly yelped again. A very small man stood there, smiling up at me.

'Who the hell are you?'

'My name's Harry Huckle. I'm a friend of Nik's.'

'He isn't here.'

'I know. It's you I came to see.'

'Why?'

'I wonder if we might have a chat?'

'Again. Why?'

'Christmas is coming. Don't you find

time flies by once we get near the end of October?'

'So?'

'Nik always comes back again for some of December.'

Okay, this was getting weird now.

'Are you Nik's father?' Somehow I didn't really think this little man could be related to Nik, but he obviously knew him well.

'No, I'm a family friend. I just know December can be a stressful time for the family, and I'm sure he hasn't told you why . . . yet.'

'He told me he goes back to help with the family business in December.'

Harry nodded his head. 'Well it's a start.'

'I don't think he'd be too pleased to hear you've come here to tell tales about his family.'

'I don't intend to tell any tales, Annie. Just to tell you he will need your help at some point, and, more importantly, your understanding. It's crucial.'

He knows my name. This is getting weirder

by the minute.

I picked up most of the hay, and separating it into smaller bundles, shook it into the manger; more to have something to do and stop my hands from shaking than anything else. The animals all looked happy enough. I gave Merlin a final pat, and walked towards the gate.

Harry didn't appear to be following, so I turned around. But as in all the best horror movies, he'd gone. Disappeared.

A random quote from *The Wizard of Oz* suddenly popped into my head. 'My! People come and go so quickly here.' It seemed appropriate somehow.

19

November

'So who's Harry Huckle?'

Nik nearly choked on his pint, gasped like a fish out of water and stared at me, grey eyes watering. 'Harry Huckle?' he croaked after a few minutes.

'Yeah, little guy, about so high.' I made a gesture with my hand.

'Harry Huckle,' Nik said again, still blinking.

'We had a chat while you were away last month. I meant to tell you before.'

Now Nik looked really worried, which worried me too. What the hell was going on?

'He works for my dad.'

'Uh huh.' Now why didn't that explanation say enough?

'He told me you would be going back to help your parents for some of December.'

Now Nik looked apologetic. 'Yes, I'm

sorry. I did mean to talk to you after Katie winkled that out of me when we were at your parents' house.'

'You don't need to look so worried, Nik,' I said. 'We've only known each other for a little while.'

'Christmas is special.'

'And there's always another one next year.'

The last thing I wanted was to scare him off. But there was something odd about this December thing, and he still hadn't told me about Harry.

'He knew my name,' I said suddenly, remembering.

Nik gave me a startled look this time. 'I probably mentioned you to Dad.'

I agreed it was the most likely explanation. Although it didn't explain how Harry knew where to find me, or even that I was me . . . he could have thought lovely Lucinda was me. I smiled at the thought.

'That's funny because . . . ?'

'I was just thinking about Lucinda Finchley-Perry.'

'Oh. Her.'

I felt more pleased than is polite, to hear the disdain in Nik's voice at the mention of her.

'She didn't take too kindly to me feeding the animals. I was going to tell you, then I decided I didn't want to tell tales on a member of your staff. But you might want to have a word with her if you need me to look after them again in December.'

He frowned. 'She's only been with us a few weeks, and I'm not at all sure she's working out.'

'I can't say I'm surprised.'

'Sally wasn't too surprised either.'

I thought about Sally, the lovely lady who worked for Nik as deputy manager. I gave him a pitying look, and signalled the barman for more drinks. Somehow I thought a discussion about Lucinda called for more alcohol.

I spotted a table for two in the corner and hurried towards it, with Nik following.

Once we'd sat down, Nik raised his

eyebrows at me over the rim of his glass. I braced myself. How did I say what I felt without looking like the new jealous girlfriend — or even worse — the new *possessive* girlfriend? He saved me the trouble, by starting the conversation again.

'She applied for the vacancy at the nursery a while ago. I didn't feel too sure about her, but I can't tell you exactly why.'

I felt sure I could, but there was no way I was going to. 'So you took her on because . . . ?'

He grimaced. 'We were pretty short-staffed at the time, and there are so many rules and regulations in childcare about the staff ratio to the number of children.' Nik took a drink from his beer. His grey eyes looked thoughtful. He glanced up at me and looked a little sheepish. 'She suggested we met for a meal in town to discuss the job.'

'She did?' Well the girl had chutzpah that's for sure. I tried to imagine myself inviting Tim out before he'd offered me a job, but no, that would never have happened. I wouldn't have asked him for a start, and actually he would never have agreed. Even if he hadn't been married with two small children.

Nik gave me a rueful grin. 'She suggested we meet at the posh Italian place in the village'

'*Pellucci's*?' I had to admit, she had taste. 'It must be about ten pounds for a cappuccino in there.'

'Naturally, I turned down her very kind invitation,' said Nik. 'And asked her instead, to come into the nursery for a second interview and to meet Sally.'

I laughed. 'I bet that went down like a lead balloon.'

'Sally wasn't convinced, and actually neither was I, if I'm honest, but after Lucinda left, we agreed to take her on for a trial period.'

'And I gather it's not been a rip-roaring success so far?'

Nik grimaced. 'Sadly, that's a bit of an understatement.'

I felt sorry for him. He'd still wanted

to give Lucinda a chance, in spite of his gut feeling. Personally, I wasn't sure I would have in his place, but I loved the fact he'd tried.

'She probably wouldn't have run up too huge a bill in Pellucci's, 'I said with a grin. 'She strikes me as one of the strictly salad brigade.'

'Oh so says the girl who nibbled at the icing on a small sliver of cake for an hour at her parents'.'

I couldn't believe he'd noticed.

'That's different,' I said. 'I'd eaten Mum's huge roast dinner, and rhubarb crumble, only a couple of hours before.'

'It didn't seem to stop Katie.'

'Katie can eat all day, every day and never put on weight,' I said crossly.

Nik leaned across the table, and picked up my hand. 'Annie, you're perfect.'

I felt my cheeks flush. 'Well . . . '

'Perfect,' he said again.

Funny how we'd strayed from the Lucinda topic — and Harry.

'To go back to the lovely Lucinda,' I said. 'What will you do?'

'Well, as she's on a trial period, as far as I'm concerned we can legally part ways any time within that period.'

I felt an enormous sense of relief to hear that. I couldn't even say why, although the thought of Lucinda interacting with small children didn't fill me with any kind of good feelings.

'What does Sally say?' I'd only met Sally once, but I'd taken to her instantly.

'She thinks we should say our good-byes.'

Good old Sally.

'She'd be a perfect match for Chris the Creep,' I said. 'Perhaps we should introduce them.'

'Chris the . . . who? What?'

'Valid questions, both,' I said. 'He was, for some reason known only to Jon, my esteemed brother-in-law, the best man at their wedding. Which I have to say, doesn't say much for the others.'

'Tall, impossibly good-looking . . . ?'

'Creep,' I said firmly. 'Of the worst and creepiest kind.'

Nik laughed aloud, and I joined in.

He looked amazing most of the time, but when he laughed, he simply oozed gorgeousness and I melted all the way down to my toes.

'When we met that day, I thought you and he . . .'

'Oh he's thought 'he and me' several times, but I can assure you it hasn't and never will happen.'

'Good. Let's introduce him to Lucinda then. They obviously deserve each other.'

It was only after I'd been home half an hour that I remembered Harry Huckle again. Nik had been clearly rattled when I started talking about him. So Harry worked in Nik's family toy business, did he? Why did he need to come and talk to me then? Their busy time of year had absolutely nothing to do with me. Although it might become a problem in the future if we stayed together — and I hoped we would.

Then of course, my imagination took off in all sorts of directions. I started imagining Nik's Dad as a sort of Marlon Brando *Godfather* character, smoking huge cigars and having members of staff 'terminated' if they didn't finish making a train set on time. That could be why Nik always had to go back to help — they'd be short-staffed what with all the terminations and everything.

By the time I went to bed, my over-active brain had gone into manic overdrive, which meant I lay awake for hours, eventually dropping off sometime in the early hours.

20

Nik stroked Rudy's neck gently. There was nothing else for it, he would have to call the vet. He'd cleaned around Rudy's eye area, but he needed the special wound spray to clear up the abscess.

'Silly old chap,' he said softly. 'I told you not to rub up against the hay.'

He pulled his phone out of his jacket pocket and called Annie. Funny how natural it felt for her to be the first person he called.

'Hi.' She answered on the second ring.

'Rudy's got an abscess on his eyelid.'

'Not the most romantic of greetings,' her amused voice came back. 'Do you need Tim to come out?'

'No, I've seen this before. I just need a Furacin wound spray if you have such a thing?'

'Hold on.'

After a muffled discussion in the

background, Annie came back.

'We have it in stock, strangely,' she said. 'There are a lot of deer in the park. I can bring it up at lunch time?'

'I'll come down now if that's all right? His eyelid looks really sore.'

'Sure. See you in a minute then.'

Nik smiled to himself. An added bonus of seeing Annie in the morning. He wondered what it would be like to see her every morning. Probably pretty fantastic.

'Nik.'

Right on cue, again. He sighed. No prizes for guessing who it might be.

'What now, Harry?'

'Have you told her yet?'

'Of course not. We've only been seeing each other for a few weeks.'

'She's a very lovely girl.'

'She is, and I don't want to blow this. It might help if you stopped hassling me all the time. I had two days of constant questions from Dad when I was back, most of which I didn't have a hope of answering.'

Nik turned away to walk towards the gate. He knew Harry wouldn't follow, so he didn't bother to continue the conversation. Talk about pressure. How on earth was he supposed to get closer to Annie with his father ringing every day and Harry turning up uninvited all the time? Showing himself to Annie had been a huge mistake on Harry's part. Luckily, she didn't appear to be the hysterical type, but even so . . .

He unlocked the car, and was about to get in when someone called him from the nursery. Lucinda. How lovely. She stalked over to him, precariously balanced on her ridiculous heels that certainly didn't look like they were in keeping with nursery staff dress code. He'd have to check.

'Lucinda?'

'Nik, I'm *so* pleased I caught you.' She put her hand on his arm and gave him a coy look.

'What's up?'

'Sarah doesn't feel well.'

'Ask Sally to send her home.'

'We'll be one short then.'

'I'll be back in half an hour.'

'We need you here now.'

'And I need to get some medicine for my sick reindeer.'

Lucinda's nostrils flared. Here was a young woman not used to being turned down. 'Can't it wait?'

Nik wondered whether she remembered who the boss was here.

'Lucinda, you are one of the junior staff here. Sally is in charge when I'm not around. Talk to her.' He got in the car, and drove away, glancing back at her in his rear view mirror. Her face was a picture. He pitied Sally, the rest of the staff and the children in the nursery for the next half an hour. He'd better be quick and not try to tempt Annie out for a quick coffee after all.

Nik went in to the surgery waiting room where the pretty receptionist looked up and smiled.

'Hello Mr Knoll.'

'Hi-er . . . ?' He was terrible with names.

'Jen.'

'Hi Jen.' He smiled back.

'Annie was going to leave out some spray for me?' Annie popped her head around the consulting room door at that moment.

'I thought I heard your dulcet tones.' She held out the spray. 'You can pay Jen.'

'Thanks. See you later?'

'You bet.' She blew him a kiss and went back into the consulting room, where a frantic yapping had started.

'Busy morning?' Nik looked around the waiting room at the motley assortment of dogs sitting with their owners, along with a few other people who sat clutching cat boxes on their knees.

'You have no idea.' Jen tapped at her keyboard and read the computer screen. 'That's fifteen pounds please.'

Nik handed over his credit card.

'Contactless?'

He nodded.

She tapped the card on her machine, and handed it back. 'You have a *reindeer*?'

'I do.'

With another smile, he walked out, leaving the receptionist gazing after him, seemingly oblivious to the scuffle that had just broken out between a Doberman and a Jack Russell.

21

Third week of November

We were sitting once again in our favourite corner of The White Hart discussing old movies, when I remembered quoting *The Wizard of Oz* to myself the night Harry disappeared. Then I remembered we hadn't really spoken about Harry since. The conversation had turned to Lucinda and Chris the Creep. How had that happened?

'So . . . how's Harry? Finished his train set yet?'

Nik looked blank. 'Train set?'

'I just have this mental picture of lots of . . . *elves* making toys for Christmas.'

I laughed at my own joke, then felt terrified because Nik appeared to be having a choking fit. Desperately trying to remember the Heimlich Manoeuver, I jumped up but he waved me back down.

'I'm fine. Fine,' he croaked.

Well I don't know about *fine*. This was

the second time that Nik had almost choked when I mentioned Harry — or anything to do with Harry. I wondered whether his father really *was* some kind of *Godfather* type gangster.

'Sorry. I laughed and drank at the same time.'

Well, I hadn't exactly noticed a lot of laughing, just an awful lot of choking.

'Are you sure you're all right?' I looked at his flushed face with concern.

'Annie, I'm fine, I promise.'

'If you're sure.'

'And Harry is being kept very busy by my father.'

'So he's not likely to pop up while you're away then?'

'Definitely not in December. So . . . about the scenery. Are you up for it?'

Another change of topic.

'Of course. What do you need?'

'A night sky with a big star painted on a very large bit of plywood?'

'Lucinda's not helping with the painting then, huh?'

'Heaven forbid. She might break a nail.'

* * *

A few days later, Nik and I were duly painting a night sky. Well we were actually covering a huge piece of plywood with dark blue paint. Some of it was going over us too, but I didn't care. The quiet of the empty nursery felt calm and very private with just the two of us, and a radio quietly playing away in the corner. I'd have been blissfully happy if November didn't appear to be whizzing by like a hurricane and there was nothing I could do to slow it down. And now the time when Nik would have to go away was getting closer. December was looming, and contrary to my usual feelings at this time of year, my festive spirit was oddly absent. Even painting scenery for Nik's Christmas show, didn't fill me with 'comfort and joy'. Even though I love to draw and paint.

'What are you doing about costumes?'

I asked, in an effort to stop myself thinking about Nik going away.

'Sally's making the dragon, but mostly the parents make the costumes for their own children.'

I sat back on my heels looking at our sky. 'We'll have to let this dry before painting the stars.'

'We'd better have coffee while we wait then.'

'Good plan.'

He leaned forward and kissed me. 'You have a splodge of blue paint on your nose. I like it.'

'I'll go and de-splodge. Where's the loo?'

He pointed to a short corridor on his right and I hurried off to check all visible areas for blue paint.

Paint-free, we sat in companionable silence in the kitchen, drinking mugs of coffee, when I caught Nik looking at me.

'What?'

'Annie, do you believe in magic?'

'As in conjurors' type magic on the stage, or Harry Potter-type magic?'

He thought for a minute. 'Real magic. So I suppose the Harry Potter kind.'

Not your everyday conversation.

'No, of course not. It's just fiction, isn't it?'

'Perhaps.'

'You're not going to tell me you believe in fairies now are you?'

'No I don't believe in fairies.' He laughed. 'Although some of my clients do, but they are only two or three years old.'

'Well let's go paint some magic stars. I'm getting hungry.'

I had to admit our sky looked pretty good once we'd painted the stars on. The star of Bethlehem shone brightly above the smaller ones, a little lopsided maybe, but I didn't think anyone would notice. We carried it over to lean against a wall to dry.

'I hope you don't get lots of little people stuck all over this in the morning,' I said.

'It will be dry by then. What do you fancy to eat?'

I was about to offer cooking for us both at my place, when my phone rang. 'Ah it's the sister who pimps me out to paint scenery.'

Nik laughed.

'Katie.'

'Hey, what are you up to?'

'Painting scenery. Your idea remember?'

'Ah. Yes. How's it going?'

'Finished, and just thinking about food.'

'Perfect. We'll see you in The Wheatsheaf then. I don't fancy cooking. Fifteen minutes.'

The phone went dead. And I *had* fancied cooking, plus I'd really fancied the rest of the evening alone with Nik. There wasn't long left until December after all.

I grimaced apologetically. 'They want us to meet them in The Wheatsheaf.'

'Let's get there first then.' Nik grabbed my hand, and pulled me towards the door.

★ ★ ★

The evening began well enough. Katie and Jon still had that newly-wed-so-in-love glow about them — being married really suited them. But then Katie began to chatter away about Christmas again, and both Nik and I grew quieter. I hadn't mentioned the imminent arrival of December and neither had he. Although strangely, Harry Huckle had. Whoever the hell Harry Huckle really was.

For the first time in years, I found I really was not looking forward to Christmas. Normally I embrace all things festive the moment we reach the first of December. I'm always the first one at work to suggest putting up early decorations too, and I always buy a real tree for my flat. I absolutely love buying Christmas presents. Planning for the big day fills me with huge excitement and I watch all the schmaltzy Christmas movies I can find on obscure TV channels. In fact, I don't think there are too many Christmas films made in the last forty years that I haven't seen at some point. Some of them I know off by heart, which is a fact Katie has always found hysterical.

Somehow, I felt this year would be different. I'd met someone I cared about, but I didn't think he would be with me for Christmas. I didn't think he'd be around for most of December either. We hadn't talked any more about it, but I felt sure we wouldn't even get to go to pre-Christmas parties together, because he might not be here. A lump formed in my throat and still Katie chattered on.

A tiny part of me hoped he might invite me to his parents' place, even though I'd never met them. But, so far, he hadn't. I really didn't want to bring up the subject of Christmas yet.

I zoned back in on the conversation because I heard my name. I blinked and looked at my sister.

'Annie, where are you this evening?'

'Here with you guys.'

'Bodily perhaps, but not mentally.'

'Sorry, busy day.'

'Anyone would think you didn't like Christmas.' She laughed and Jon joined in. Then she turned to Nik. 'Annie decorates the vets' surgery *and* the waiting room, her flat, *anything* and *anywhere* she can. She'll decorate your paddock too, I expect, and put red bows and tinsel on all the animals. I've never known anyone love Christmas more than Annie.'

I thought Nik would go even quieter at that, but to my surprise he grinned his normal heart-melting grin at me, and said, 'I love Christmas too.'

I really would have to pluck up the courage to talk about the December thing soon.

22

First week of December

It was almost time for the dress rehearsal, and all the children were excited, verging on the hyper. Tom and Danny made adorable elves, and Nik grinned as they raced around the festively decorated main room, their false pointy ears flapping, and cheeks flushed pink with excitement. Sally had put little daubs of blusher on their cheeks too, and he really hoped Danny's mother didn't object tomorrow when they did the show for the parents and grandparents.

A flutter of fairies suddenly skipped into the room. Sally had obviously worked her own magic on them too. The parents had done everyone proud this year; the costumes they'd made (or hired) were absolutely gorgeous. His and Annie's scenery looked almost professional now it was in place, even with the lopsided Star of Bethlehem, although Nik didn't think anyone else would notice it was crooked.

Sally came in with her script attached to a clipboard, looking every inch the dedicated producer. She clapped her hands above the bedlam and all the children stopped to listen. Nik thought again how lucky he was to have her working with him at the nursery. All the children and their parents adored her.

The rehearsal went as well as could be expected with twenty excited children in fancy dress who were already in 'it's December so it must be nearly Christmas' mode. Although there was very nearly a disaster when the dragon almost tore itself in half because its tail end suddenly decided to go off in a different direction to the front half, and only Nik's speedy intervention saved its demise.

Tom lost an ear and the dragon's many feet trod on it, meaning Sally would have to make a new one in time for tomorrow. But other than that, Nik had to admit, it looked pretty good, and the 'baby Jesus' only got dropped once by Mary, as opposed to the several times the poor doll had suffered in the beginning of rehearsals.

The three 'Christmas trees' had been more than a bit competitive with each other and there'd been a slight tussle for centre stage, which could potentially become a problem tomorrow. Nik had had to stand between Tree Number One and Tree Number Two in order to explain they weren't really supposed to stand at the front of the stage for the whole play, but only when they first came on to say their poem. They were then supposed to move to the side, to make room for the dragon, and they shouldn't ever stand in front of Mary and the baby Jesus at all. He didn't think any of the Christmas trees were too impressed by that, and they all looked a bit sulky when they moved reluctantly to stand to one side. Their behaviour didn't bode well for the big performance tomorrow. It would appear some little Christmas trees fully intended to steal the show.

By the time parents started to arrive to collect their budding Oscar winners, the children's faces had been washed free of blusher and they were dressed in their normal clothes again. Nik and Sally started hanging the little costumes up with the help of two of the other girls. It would have been nice if Lucinda had deigned to help, but she'd suddenly remembered an 'urgent' appointment with the hygienist. Nik couldn't help feeling the sooner they parted company with her the better it would be for everyone. But he was really looking forward to the show tomorrow. Some of the little ones had definite star quality, and he felt sure the audience would be very appreciative no matter what happened.

★ ★ ★

The next day, Nik wheeled and coaxed Rudy into the nursery building. He wished Annie could have taken the afternoon off for the nativity play. He could have brought Merlin in as well then.

The little pony clearly adored Annie, and followed her everywhere whenever he could — without biting too. Annie had forbidden Nik to allow the kids to feed him tidbits. She said it made him snappy, and he had certainly been much calmer and friendlier since. Nik could hardly believe the change in him.

The arrival of several parents, interrupted his train of thought. Rudy was admired and petted, which he seemed to really enjoy. He blinked ridiculously long dark eyelashes at everyone who cooed over him.

Tom's mum whooshed in just before the start of the play, smiling apologetically over at Nik. He waved back and, handing Rudy's halter rope to Sally, he went to stand in front of the starry sky he'd painted with Annie.

'Good afternoon everyone,' he began, and all the rustlings and whispers died away. 'Thank you all for coming today, the kids have really been looking forward to it — especially the dragon.'

There was a ripple of laughter.

'But I have to warn you to watch out for the Christmas trees. They are a little . . . unusual. Please enjoy the show.'

The audience applauded. It appeared everyone was happy to start Christmas in the first week of December.

Nik nodded over to Sarah sitting at the piano. She started to play 'Silent Night', and the children filed in, their faces aglow with excitement — and possibly too much blusher, applied again by an enthusiastic Sally. Tom had a new ear to replace the one trampled by dragon feet, and every so often he forgot where he was supposed to be, and stopped to wave at his mother instead — but judging from the ecstatic look of pride on her face, it didn't matter one bit.

The children sang their hearts out, the bad Christmas trees pushed and shoved each other for the centre stage spot, but the real hit of the afternoon was the dragon. A twelve-legged dragon no less, with each child holding up a letter which, when they stood in a straight line, spelt 'dragon'. The applause was almost

154

deafening and startled Rudy. Unfortunately, when everyone came back together for a final bow, the children dressed as the dragon returned in the wrong order and spelt 'nogard'. Most people thought this was a deliberate joke for the parents, so Nik felt no harm had been done to his production. Although he seriously doubted Andrew Lloyd Webber needed to worry.

By the time parents and children had left, and they'd cleared up, it was getting quite late.

'Good job everyone,' he said, as his staff filed out of the door looking exhausted. 'See you tomorrow.'

He felt relieved he'd taken Rudy back outside earlier as the young reindeer had started to get a little fractious with all the noise, and he didn't want him upset. His eyelid had cleared up perfectly, which was a huge relief. But all the animals needed feeding now.

He started towards the main door, and his thoughts turned to the gift he'd had specially made for Annie. He hoped she'd like it. Jewellery was such a personal gift, and they really hadn't been together very long. Would it seem weird to her? Suppose she thought it too soon and too pushy of him to buy her jewellery? He thought she'd like it; he knew how much she loved Christmas after all, and she obviously loved animals too. One of his father's craftsmen had made it, and his work was second to none, so he had no worries about the quality of the piece. It should be perfect. Then he wondered when would be the right time to actually give it to her.

The air outside felt crisp and fresh as he made his way across the paddock. Merlin looked up and whinnied softly.

'Sorry matey, no Annie today,' said Nik. 'She's still at work ... and hello Harry what a surprise.' He allowed sarcasm to tinge his words, as he went to the shed to get the feed.

Harry stayed sitting on the fence, and watched Nik moving around the bigger animals, putting the feed into the mangers and topping up the water trough.

'How are your December plans coming along?' Harry asked finally, after a considerable silence.

'It's the 8th of December tomorrow,' said Nik heavily. 'I will be back on the 11th. End of story.'

'And Annie?'

'Annie is none of your business, and I'd thank you not to appear again when I'm not here. I don't want the poor girl frightened to death.'

'I'm trying to help.'

Nik felt his anger rising. 'Well you aren't helping. You're making everything more difficult to explain. Now please go back to Dad and tell him the same.'

'I'm sorry you feel like this . . . '

'No. You're not. You're not even thinking about me, and even less about the effect all this is having on Annie.'

'Nik . . . the magic . . . '

But Nik interrupted him. 'Yeah, yeah, me and Dumbledore.' By the time he'd taken a deep breath, the little man had done his disappearing act again. Nik ran a hand through his hair and frowned at the empty space where Harry had been. How he wished he was just an ordinary bloke, someone who could spend Christmas Eve with the girl he felt pretty sure he loved, appreciating the real magic of Christmas. Not some freak of a bloke with probably one of the weirdest families ever. He wondered whether Annie would ever accept his family, or if she'd just reject him *and* them once she knew.

23

Nik and I were sitting at a very secluded table in salubrious Pellucci's. He'd said because he would be away for two weeks, and possibly longer, we should have our Christmas Eve early.

I didn't feel inclined to argue, but to be honest, I didn't feel much like celebrating either. Even though we haven't been together very long, the thought of being without him for any length of time made me feel unhappy.

Nik pushed a beautifully wrapped Christmas present across the table towards me.

'You can open it now,' he said. 'I want you to.'

'But . . . ' I'd been brought up never to open Christmas presents before the day.

It almost felt dishonest.

'Please.'

It was the please that did it. I ripped

off the paper to reveal a long dark blue box. I opened it, and inside lay a beautiful silver reindeer on a chain, nestling against blue velvet.

'It's beautiful.' I lifted the pendant carefully out from its box. The delicate silverwork was exquisite, and the reindeer caught the reflection of the restaurant's Christmas lights, giving it an almost ethereal glow. 'Nik, thank you — so much.'

'Wear it now.' He smiled. 'Here let me . . .'

He fastened the pendant around my neck, where it continued to glow.

'It really suits you.' He sat back down, looking very pleased with himself.

'I love it,' I said. 'But it does make my gift to you look a bit ordinary.'

Thank heavens I actually had a present for him — I had toyed with the idea of not buying him anything. New relationships are a minefield when it comes to present buying. Not just what to get, but whether to get. Eventually, after much trudging around shops and suffering from considerable angst, I'd decided on a classy leather wallet with his initials embossed on the front. I'd noticed his current wallet looked in danger of collapse, and I felt wary of buying anything too personal. The new relationship thing again.

I passed the gift across to him.

At that moment, the waitress appeared to take our order.

'I love your pendant,' she said. 'It has a kind of Christmassy glow about it.' Nik continued to look pleased with himself.

'Having an early Christmas?'

'Something like that,' I said, ordering the shrimp and crab fettuccini.

Nik ordered the same, but added garlic bread and salad for both of us, and a bottle of wine.

The waitress hurried away and I watched Nik open his present.

'Annie it's amazing, thank you. How did you know I needed a new wallet?'

He took his old wallet out, and started moving everything into the new one. I looked pointedly at the old wallet. The edges were frayed, the lining torn and some of the pockets looked more than a little sorry for themselves, and no longer much like pockets either.

'Fair point.' He grinned, and leaned across the table to kiss me.

'After this meal, I'll definitely be on a diet,' I said.

'Apparently this place does the best tiramisu in the south east,' said Nik, 'and what do you mean *diet*?'

'Well we have eaten out a lot since we met,' I said. 'Normally I would only have a tuna salad or something in the evening and then a roast at Mum's on Sunday.'

'I don't want to come back to a waif and stray.'

I sighed. 'I'd love to be waif-like, but I seriously doubt it will ever happen. I like my food too much. And I promise not to stray.'

'Good.'

The waitress returned with the wine, and poured some for Nik to taste. I noticed she kept staring at my pendant, and I glanced down. The sparkling reflections from the Christmas tree lights looked brighter than ever, glowing and shimmering in the silver body of the reindeer.

'Where did you get it?' she asked.

Nik answered. 'A family friend is a jeweller. He's really exceptional, and I asked him to make it.'

Wow. A specially-commissioned piece of jewellery. I wondered if Harry Huckle had made it, but decided I wouldn't mention his name again, at the risk of making Nik choke.

We clinked our glasses together, and I watched the restaurant's flickering candlelight glow through the deep red of the wine. I hadn't even had a drink yet, but I felt slightly light-headed. Perhaps I *needed* a drink.

I wondered whether Nik would discuss the reason behind his return to his parents' place, but I didn't want to spoil the mood of the evening.

'Annie you look so lovely tonight. How am I ever going to cope without you?'

Okay, so it looked like I would have to

be the brave one.

'It's not forever,' I said. 'Will you be back for New Year's Eve?'

'Absolutely.' He took hold of my hand and played with the bangle on my wrist that Katie had bought me. 'And we're going to party to make up for lost time.'

'Deal.' I nodded.

Our food arrived, and I decided the diet whilst Nik was away was a must.

Apart from New Year's Eve, and Christmas Day of course.

Pellucci's reputation for the best tiramisu in the south east was also not exaggerated in the slightest. It melted in the mouth, and the alcoholic content would have failed a breathalyser. We didn't speak much during the tiramisu, just the occasional 'mmm' and 'umm'.

Finally I leant back in my chair. 'I think I've just eaten my whole body weight in Italian cuisine.'

Nik grinned. 'Me too.'

The waitress cleared the plates and came back with cappuccinos. 'Sambuca? Limoncello?'

'Neither, but thank you.' I shook my head. 'I'm not sure I can stand up as it is.'

I kept glancing at Nik as I drank my coffee. He looked thoughtful, and I wondered what he was thinking about.

He asked for the bill and refused to let me contribute. Knowing how over-priced the place was, I felt terrible, but he was adamant. He said it was his idea, and therefore his treat.

We walked up the street towards the taxi rank, hands linked and chatting easily. I really was dreading him going away. I'd become used to being half of a couple faster than I'd ever have thought possible. I've always been independent and happy in my own company. Now I felt miserable at the thought of even one weekend alone. I gave myself a mental shake. Pathetic. Then realised Nik was talking to me.

'Sorry?'

'I won't come back with you, Annie. I have to make a really early start. Will you be okay to see to the animals in the morning?'

'Of course.'

I looked up at him, watching the glints in his eyes. They almost looked like the Christmas lights from the restaurant, except there weren't any Christmas lights on this street yet.

He leaned down and kissed me, pulling me closer. I wound my arms around his neck, as he deepened the kiss.

When he drew back, he touched my face gently. 'I'll miss you.'

'Me too,' I said softly.

He opened the door of the first cab, and reluctantly I got in, my hand touching the silver reindeer around my neck. He noticed the gesture and smiled, blowing me a kiss. He shut the door and the taxi pulled away. When I turned around in the seat to wave again, he was nowhere to be seen. He must have grabbed another cab.

★ ★ ★

I let myself into the silent apartment. I used to love solitude, but now I just felt lonely, and actually if I'm honest, slightly bereft.

I took off the pendant, and laid it carefully back in its box. It could have been the mixture of wine I'd drunk, the alcohol in the tiramisu or simply wishful thinking, but I could have sworn the silver reindeer glinted back at me with all the iridescence and beauty of a myriad of Christmas tree lights . . .

24

Second week of December

The second week of December brought a thick frost and a cruel biting wind. I trudged across Nik's paddock before work, muttering to myself about the weather and absentee boyfriends.

My feet felt frozen solid, in spite of my thermal socks. I stamped them in a parody of a rain dance once I reached the animals' enclosure.

Rudy and Gertie watched with a certain detached interest, whilst Merlin eyed me with disapproval. Clearly not a fan of my dance moves.

'You can always join in, Merlin,' I said.

He snickered his little pony laugh.

I continued with my usual banter to the animals as I sorted out food for everyone, broke the ice on the water trough and saw to the small animals in hutches. I had my routine down to a fine art now, which was just as well as Rudy,

Gertie and Merlin tended to gang up on me if I took too long.

I made a fuss of the 'three amigos' before turning to leave, keeping a wary eye out for the mysterious Harry Huckle, just in case he turned up again. Thankfully he didn't. Too busy making toys probably.

When I neared the main gate, I noticed a tiny blond figure standing there. He seemed to be crying.

'Hello?' I called when I reached him. 'Are you okay?'

A cherubic, tear-stained face with enormous blue eyes looked up at me. 'Can't get back in.'

'In where?'

He pointed back at the nursery.

'What are you doing out here in the cold?'

'Postman left the door open. Wanted to see Merlin.'

The poor little mite. I had a horrid feeling they hadn't even missed him in the nursery yet. 'What's your name?'

'Tommy.'

'Okay Tommy, would you like to put my gloves on?'

Serious blue eyes looked at me again. 'Too big.'

'Yes I know, but they'll warm up your hands really quickly. And then we'll go back inside.'

'Yes please.'

I pulled off my gloves and wiggled them on to his tiny hands. They felt like little blocks of ice. Anything could have happened to little Tommy out here on his own. It didn't really bear thinking about. He could have wandered out on to the main road, or hurt himself trying to see Merlin. The little pony was friendlier these days, but he could easily have kicked Tommy by mistake.

I held my hand out to Tommy and he put his enormously gloved hand clumsily into mine.

'Inside?' he said hopefully.

'You bet.'

The main doors to the nursery opened when I pressed the entry buzzer and luckily it was Sally sitting behind the reception desk now. She looked up as the door opened.

'Can I help . . . ?' She almost did a double-take when she saw Tommy. 'What . . . ?'

'Apparently, the postman didn't close the door properly, and Tommy here went outside to see Merlin. Luckily I was there feeding the animals. I don't think he's been outside too long, but his hands are frozen.'

'How? Oh God, he must have slipped out when I went to the loo. Thank heavens you were outside . . . I'm sorry . . . we have met before, haven't we?'

'Yes we have. Once. I'm Annie — Nik's, er — girlfriend. I'm looking after the animals while he's away.'

Sally's attractive face broke into a beam. 'Of course. How lovely to see you again, Annie.' She held a hand out and we shook hands. 'Your hands are freezing too.'

'Not half as freezing as poor little Tommy's. I put my gloves on him, but I think he needs a hot drink?'

Sally immediately went in to efficient childcare mode, and bustled off to get hot drinks and a blanket. Only minutes later, Tommy was sitting in Sally's chair, huddled in a blanket and sipping hot chocolate from a child's mug with a lid.

'I'm nearly three,' he said in the sudden silence.

'And a very big, brave boy you are too,' said Sally.

'I'm not a bad boy for going outside, am I?'

'No, of course you're not,' said Sally firmly. 'You're always a very good boy. But you must never go outside without a grown-up again.

She handed me a mug of hot chocolate. 'You'd better drink this before you go to work.'

I accepted the drink gratefully, wrapping my frozen hands around the mug to thaw them out.

At that moment Lucinda strode out of the nursery, her eyes narrowing when she saw me.

'What's the farm help doing in here?'

she said nastily.

Sally spoke before I could. 'Annie is Nik's girlfriend, and has just rescued little Tommy here from hypothermia. Didn't you miss him?'

Lucinda's green eyes flashed in anger. She looked at me as if I'd just crawled out from under a rock. 'You have no right to interfere with anything that has less than four legs.'

I stood up to my full height, and stared her straight in the eyes. She took a step backwards.

'Whilst *you*, *Ms* Finchley-Perry should have noticed a small child in your care had gone missing.' She opened and closed her mouth, giving a passable imitation of a goldfish, and I held up a hand.

'I haven't finished,' I snapped. 'I don't think you're fit to work with frogs, let alone small children, but I agree it's none of my business, so let's agree to disagree, shall we?'

Not surprisingly Lucinda backed down when faced with someone who didn't crumble under her tactics. She spun on her ill-advisable heels, turned and made for the staff room.

'Sally, I'm going home now,' she said, when she returned with her coat and bag.

Sally raised an eyebrow. 'I'll mark it on your timesheet. We'll see you in the morning.'

Personally, I would have stayed to talk things over with Sally myself, because to be fair, Lucinda wasn't the only person on duty in the nursery. Someone should really have noticed Tommy was missing, so there didn't seem any reason for Lucinda to take all the blame. I almost felt sorry for her. Almost. But then I'm the kind of person who likes to solve problems. We're all different, I suppose. It was anyone's guess whether Lucinda would actually turn up for work in the morning. How I wish this hadn't happened when I was here. I had no idea what Nik would think about it all.

'I shall report back to Nik myself.' A voice from the doorway spoke before I could say any more. Harry Huckle of course. Possibly having run out of trains to paint.

Lucinda goggled at him in disbelief. 'Who the hell are you?'

'That's a rude word,' piped up Tommy.

I think we'd all forgotten him momentarily.

Sally snorted into her hot chocolate. 'Nice to see you again Harry. How are you?' She looked over at the little man, who winked back at her.

'Well in that case she really should go home. What do you think Tommy?' I turned to him, feeling relieved his little face was a healthy colour again.

'Home,' he said with a solemn nod of his blond head.

Harry pushed open the main door, and a blast of freezing air whooshed in. I shivered.

'Miss . . . ?' He gestured for Lucinda to leave.

With a final murderous glare at me, she swept out, without looking back.

'Thanks Harry,' I said. He'd gone again, of course. I wondered whether he'd tell tales on me — overstepping every mark in the book, interfering in something I had no business interfering in. I turned to Sally. 'I am so sorry,' I began. 'I shouldn't have spoken out of turn like that.'

To my relief, she burst out laughing. 'Don't be,' she said. 'She did very little actual work to be perfectly honest.' Sally collected our empty mugs. 'I think Sarah has a list of girls who do part-time nursery work, in the event Lucinda doesn't grace us with her presence in the morning. Don't worry, we'll ring round.'

'You think she won't come back?' Now I felt truly horrified. 'Nik will be furious.'

'He'll be fine,' said Sally, patting my arm.

'Can I play with Danny now?' Tommy threw off his blanket.

'Of course you can,' said Sally. 'Shall we give Annie her gloves back first?'

She pulled my gloves from Tommy's proffered hands, and gave them back to me. I noticed she ran a professional touch over both hands to make sure they were warm.

She saw me watching. 'He's fine.'

'I'd better get to work,' I said. 'I'm going to be late.'

'Thanks for what you did Annie.'

'Pleasure,' I grinned. 'See you, Tommy.'

'Bye Annie.' Tommy ran over and hugged me round the legs before taking hold of Sally's hand as she took him back in to the main play area.

Getting in my car, I glanced down at the dashboard clock. The Tommy and Lucinda interlude had taken only fifteen minutes. It felt much longer. Strangely, I was only five minutes late for work, and I still beat Tim.

25

16 December

'You sent one of his staff home?' Katie stared at me with a mixture of disbelief and admiration. 'Annie, you're bonkers.'

'Yeah I know.' I gave an apologetic shrug of my shoulders. 'But she didn't even miss little Tommy. He could have got run over — anything could have happened. And to be fair, she's the one who said she was going home.'

'Think I know her vaguely,' Katie continued, obviously thinking aloud. 'Her father's a councillor and a property developer; filthy rich of course. Lucinda went to Montague's — you know — the private school? Daddy dearest thought the school would get her into a decent uni, but she didn't get into uni, so she went to business college.'

'Well if that's you knowing someone vaguely, I dread to think what you'd know about them if you knew them well,'

I observed dryly.

We were having Saturday lunch at the new bistro on the edge of the village, and I'd been trying to ignore the mouth-watering selection of home-baked cakes and scones on offer. I was desperately trying to stick to my 'December diet', and felt determined Nik would come back to a svelte and sophisticated Annie on New Year's Eve. Well, a thinner one anyway.

Katie continued as if I hadn't spoken. 'Then she changed her mind about working in business, and went to train as a nursery nurse.'

I raised my eyebrows. 'She's *trained*?'

'Well, she must have qualified mustn't she? Or Nik wouldn't have given her a job in the first place.'

'Even he didn't seem to know how or why he'd given her the job,' I said.

'Probably fluttered her eyelashes and gave him the 'come on' act.'

I spluttered out a laugh. If anyone could flutter eyelashes and get whatever she wanted from whomever she wanted, my money was on Katie. She smiled without a trace of self-consciousness.

'Do you think Nik will be mad if she doesn't come back to work?'

'I'm sure he'll thank you,' said Katie.

'I hope you're right.'

I'd had several sleepless nights over the Lucinda incident. I felt responsible, and a little niggling part of me still felt a bit sorry for her. Everyone makes mistakes and surely nobody could possibly be as mean as she appeared to be. Most people have one redeeming feature, after all. Although try as I might, I failed to see what hers could be.

I'd tried texting Nik countless times to confess, but never received an answer. Just where did his parents live? Outer Mongolia? Obviously it must be somewhere really remote where it was impossible to get a phone signal. I hadn't heard from him at all, and neither had the mysterious Harry Huckle turned up since the time he appeared at the nursery. It felt as if the pair of them had completely disappeared off the face of the earth.

'Hello — earth to Annie . . .' Katie

wafted a toasted teacake under my nose. It smelt really good. 'Want to share this?'

'Oh yes.' Half a teacake couldn't have *too* many calories, could it? Less than a whole one anyway.

Lunch with Katie definitely cheered me up, but I really missed Nik. I wondered about the 'radio silence' too. Trust me to fall for a good-looking guy with a mysterious family who had weird rules for December, and a very short helper with a habit of turning up when you least expected him. And disappeared soon after. You couldn't make it up.

Later, I sat on my sofa staring unseeingly at the TV. We were now in the middle of December, although it felt like this week had been going on *forever*.

I wished Nik would call, text, WhatsApp . . . *anything*. I was beginning to feel like he didn't actually exist at all, and maybe I'd invented him. With the weirdness of the last few weeks, I could believe anything. I knew I was being ever so slightly pathetic too, which wasn't helping. Not like me at all. I needed to *do* something. Then suddenly I realised I hadn't even decorated my flat for Christmas. That was very unlike me. But New Year's Eve was still officially Christmas, and Nik would definitely be back then. *Wouldn't* he? And I really needed a tree before everywhere was sold out. There were places all over town selling real trees, and most were open until at least nine in the evening now. I grabbed my bag and coat, and headed downstairs.

Now I absolutely love going to buy a Christmas tree. It means Christmas is nearly here at last. A tiny part of me wanted to buy a huge *monster* of a tree, but I knew I'd never get it up the stairs. Not single-handedly anyway.

The first place I tried only *had* huge monster trees left. Forget the stairs, none of those trees would even fit in my car. In fact, most of them were bigger than my car.

I drove into the Ashley Wood garden centre on the edge of town. It was packed. Trust me to pick an evening when their Santa was there. I avoided the

Grotto, where a couple of extremely tall elves were haphazardly trying to make twenty or so very excited small children calm down and form an orderly queue. I didn't envy them their job one bit. Perhaps Harry Huckle could get a job here?

The Christmas tree section was much bigger than the last place, and particularly well-organised. Trees were graded by size and species. I found the perfect tree in seconds. And in under ten minutes, I had the base of the tree trimmed, and put through the tunnel thingy that squished it inside a giant hair net. Or tree net. Having paid, I triumphantly wheeled the trolley with the tree back to my car.

'Need a hand, Miss?'

I spun around. '*Nik?* What? How?' My heart did a double somersault and rendered me speechless.

He laughed and grabbed me around the waist. 'I needed to check on something for the nursery and there's no way I could leave without seeing you.'

'How . . . ?'

'Your Mum gave me Katie's number, and she said you'd almost certainly be out getting a tree if you weren't at home. This is the third place I tried. And here you are.'

I flung my arms around his neck. 'I'm so sorry.'

He pushed me away gently, holding on to my arms. 'For?'

'For the Lucinda incident.'

To my relief, he gave a loud shout of laughter. 'Thank goodness one of us had the guts to have a strong word with her. You are my hero.'

'It wasn't my place to . . .'

'No it wasn't, but who cares?'

'You aren't mad?'

Sparkling grey eyes looked down into mine. 'Annie, that woman has caused more trouble between the staff in a few weeks than anyone else has ever. I was going to keep her on until Christmas because it seemed the right thing to do. She's on a probation contract until then, but I wouldn't have kept her on. Tommy might not have been found for hours if it

184

hadn't been for you.'

I felt embarrassed. 'I don't think it would have been hours before anyone noticed . . . '

'Tommy could have got pneumonia.' Nik gently pushed my hair back from my face and leaned down to kiss me. 'Tommy's parents want to meet you to say thank you.'

'Is that why you came back?'

I wondered how he'd known about the incident, and then remembered Harry saying he'd report back to Nik straight away. Obviously he'd done just that. Well — good old Harry.

'Partly.'

'How long are you here for?'

'Two or three days.'

Better than nothing, and a wonderful surprise too. I feasted my eyes on his face, the sculpted cheekbones, those incredible eyes and his very luscious lips.

'I missed you.'

He smiled. 'Thank goodness. I was worried you might have made off with Chris the Creep.'

'Perish the thought.' I shuddered. 'He's reserved for Lucinda, remember?'

'He might be too good for her.'

I chose not to comment, although I secretly agreed.

Nik looked at the tree in my trolley. 'You couldn't find a bigger one?'

'I was tempted by all the bigger ones actually,' I said. 'But they were all bigger than my car.'

'I think we might have to load this one into my car anyway.' Looking at the tree again, I thought he could be right. 'Good job you're here then.'

'It is.'

He wheeled my trolley over to his estate car, and opened the boot. Leaning in, he released the catch to collapse the back seats. The tree fitted in perfectly. Not only that, but the boot closed easily too. I felt sure my boot would never have closed.

'I'll follow you home.' He winked.

Probably the most fantastic words I'd heard in a long time.

Nik not only carried the tree easily upstairs, he fixed it into the metal stand, and managed to get it to stand up straight too. Whenever I did it, the tree always developed a drunken tilt. Or maybe that was just Katie and I after a few beers.

Even without decorations, the tree looked fabulous, standing proudly in my bay window, and it filled the room with the fresh smell of forests and pine. Personally, I never understood how people could prefer artificial trees when they could have a real one like this.

'It's absolutely perfect.' I sighed happily.

'Shall we decorate it together?' Nik touched a bough of the tree almost reverently. 'Where are your decorations?'

'On top of my wardrobe. I'll get them.'

The thought of decorating the tree with Nik filled me with indescribable happiness. Okay, so he wouldn't be here for the actual day, but it really was only a day, and Christmas was a whole season after all (which according to Selfridges started in August). Plus every time I looked at the tree I'd think of him. And now I sounded like a love-struck teenager.

I went in to the bedroom, and hauled a chair over to the wardrobe. Every year I always thought I really should find somewhere more accessible to store the decorations, but when it was time to put them away again for another year, they always ended up on top of the wardrobe. Clambering onto the chair, I reached as far as I could across the length of the top of the wardrobe and attempted to grab the giant plastic bag of lights and decorations. Yugh! A year's dust met my groping fingers. Shuddering, I hoped there weren't any spiders lurking up there.

'I don't want to go all macho on you, especially as you are my hero, but I am taller.' Nik spoke from the doorway.

I turned around, and would have fallen off the chair, except Nik was there wrapping his arms around me, just in time to prevent an accident.

'And now you're *my* hero,' I said.

He set me down on the floor, keeping his arms around me. 'We should celebrate.'

'Decorate first, celebrations afterwards.'

'Maybe some wine while we decorate?'

'You are a really bad influence.'

'My mission in life.'

It took a while to untangle the lights, but I have to say Nik was unusually adept at sorting them out. Although he probably had to decorate the nursery for lots of different events, so he'd be pretty handy with lights and stuff.

I managed to find a reasonable-looking bottle of Rioja stashed in one of my cupboards, and even found two wine glasses that almost matched. They looked a bit dusty, so I hurriedly washed and dried them. I couldn't remember the last time I'd opened a bottle of wine in the flat. I usually drank either an occasional beer or shedloads of coffee when I was here alone.

'I hope it's all right.' I looked at the

contents of the glass dubiously, as I handed it to Nik. 'I don't know how long this bottle's been in the cupboard.'

'I'm sure it's fine,' he said, clinking his glass to mine. 'Let me be the first to wish you a Happy Christmas, Annie.'

'Thank you, and a Happy Christmas to you too,' I replied. 'What will you be doing?'

'On the day?' He took a gulp of wine, and set the glass on the low table nearby. He gave me a shrewd look.

I couldn't believe I'd just come out with the question. I'm obviously more like Katie than I thought.

'Sorry. It's none of my business.' I swigged down a large amount of wine in one go and very nearly choked. 'Sorry,' I said again, my eyes watering.

He looked amused, and came to take the glass from me. He put it next to his on the table and brushed away the tears on my cheek caused by coughing.

'I'm sorry too,' he said. 'I don't mean to be Mr Mysterious. But I don't want you to think I'm a raving lunatic either, or to drive you away.'

'You won't drive me away,' I said. 'Unless you want to.'

His glance fell on the silver reindeer pendant he'd given me. He held it gently between his thumb and forefinger, and smiled at me.

'Have you noticed anything unusual about this?' he asked.

'Sometimes it looks as if it's full of Christmas lights,' I said. 'But to be fair, I have often worn it near Christmas lights, like now.'

Nik looked pleased at my answer. He turned me back to look at the tree. 'We haven't turned on any lights yet.'

26

I looked down at my pendant. Sure enough, the reindeer glowed with thousands of tiny lights, shimmering back up at me.

'How?'

'Do you remember me asking you if you believed in magic?'

'Yes.'

'This pendant holds some very special Christmas magic.'

I looked back up at Nik. He looked serious, although I still thought he had to be joking.

'And just how did you come by this magic?'

'Now *that* is a very good question.'

I still couldn't be sure whether or not he was serious. 'How?' I insisted.

He took a deep breath. 'My family go back a very long way. The jeweller who made this pendant is an old family friend. The lights are only seen in the pendant if . . . ' He paused.

'If?'

Somehow I knew instinctively the answer would be important. And I also knew it would be very likely to affect everything in the future. Especially my future.

'If the person wearing the pendant, is definitely the right person for me.' He looked more than a little embarrassed now. 'My — er — soul mate, if you like.'

Not exactly the answer I'd been expecting. 'Soul mate? What does that even mean?'

'Actually, I'm not sure.' He gave me an apologetic smile.

'Who makes up these crazy rules? Or is it just a way of getting rid of unwanted girlfriends?'

I hadn't meant to say that. And I immediately wished I could take the words back. Me and my big mouth. He didn't answer. Feeling like the biggest prat in the world, I walked over to the sofa. I definitely needed to sit down before I fell down. And I needed more wine. Very possibly a *lot* more wine. Who or what decided about a person's soul mate? And what exactly *was* a soul mate anyway? Stuff straight out of fantasy fiction, that's what. I didn't see myself as anyone's *soul mate* that's for sure. Sounded weird to me. And more than a little presumptuous. Did it mean I would have to become a Stepford Wife because of a piece of jewellery? I glanced over at Nik as I sat down. He still looked uncomfortable. Strange, because he didn't actually *look* mad, or even the tiniest bit drunk. He just looked the same as always — gorgeous.

Reaching the sofa safely, without falling, fainting or speaking any of my nonsensical thoughts aloud, I sat down, and picked up my glass. When I held it up in front of me, hundreds of beautiful coloured lights twinkled in the wine — the same lights which shone out from my pendant. If I didn't know any better, I'd think I was already very drunk.

'Annie?' Nik looked concerned now,

and sat in the armchair opposite. 'Are you okay?'

'I really have no idea.' I took a gulp of wine. 'I think I need to get drunk in order to process all this information.'

'Annie . . . I . . . I love you.'

I stared at him. I hadn't expected that either. Visions of being a Stepford Wife faded instantly. He *loved* me?

'I know everything's happened really fast, but I loved you from the moment you knocked me over in the car park.'

Relief flooded through me. He didn't want to get rid of me either. Yet.

I laughed weakly, and took another mouthful of wine. 'Swept you off your feet, huh?'

'Literally.'

I finished my glass of wine and reached for the bottle. 'I'm seriously crap at this kind of conversation,' I said.

'Me too.'

He took the bottle from me, and poured me some more wine. I picked up my glass straight away, and took another large mouthful. I was beginning to feel better. A little light-headed, but better. I looked at his concerned face.

'Don't be worried,' I said, waggling the glass at him. I finished the glass and poured another.

'Have you eaten tonight?'

'Nope.'

He muttered something that sounded a bit rude from where I was sitting.

I took another gulp of wine. Then good sense prevailed in spite of the woozy sensation flooding my body. *Put. The. Glass. Down. Annie.* I put the glass down. Nik moved it out of my reach.

'Sorry.' I seemed to keep apologising tonight. 'I had to drink a bit more because I need to tell you I love you too.' *Oh Annie — where did that come from?*

'Okay, I've told you, you've told me, and we're all good. So can you lay off the booze long enough for me to go and grab a takeaway?'

'Sure.'

I curled up on the sofa after Nik left to fetch a Chinese. Luckily I'd had the good sense to lend him my keys. The lack of sleep, no food and the sudden influx of red wine, plus this incredibly strange evening were all taking their toll.

I thought I'd close my eyes just for a minute or two, until Nik came back.

27

Nik fidgeted in the queue at the Chinese takeaway. Unfortunately it was a Saturday evening, and the world and his wife had decided to get a Chinese takeaway. He felt worried about Annie. She hadn't appeared too impressed with the first part of his explanation, and it wasn't exactly a good sign. Now he only had two days at the most, to tell her the rest, because tonight had just been the tip of the iceberg. She would almost certainly think him barking mad — there was no way she wouldn't. But with a bit of luck, perhaps she'd still love him anyway? He could hope. He also hoped she didn't call the police on him.

Nik stared at the aquarium on the wall, and a bored-looking stripey fish stared back, its mouth opening and closing in hypnotic fashion.

He continued to mentally argue with

himself until he reached the front of the queue at last. He put in his order, took a number and sat to wait for his food. At times like this, he wished he smoked — or vaped — so he could walk about outside looking angst-ridden, vaping and talking on his mobile, like a lot of the other guys. But as he did neither of those things, he was forced to sit on a narrow wooden bench with a number. He hoped Annie was all right.

Half an hour later, Nik let himself into an ominously silent flat.

'Annie?'

No answer.

He almost ran into the living room, and skidded to a halt at the sight of Annie curled up on the sofa. She'd appeared exhausted earlier, and clearly drinking wine on an empty stomach had knocked her out. She looked adorable.

He set the containers down on the table, and went over to the sofa. Squatting down next to her, he gently ran a hand over her shining hair, and brushed the backs of his fingers down her smooth cheek. Her thick dark eyelashes cast tiny shadows on her flushed cheeks, and her lips definitely needed kissing.

Feeling like the prince in *Sleeping Beauty*, he leaned over and kissed her softly. She sat up with a start, almost head-butting him on the way. He lost his balance and fell over backwards, banging his head on the leg of the armchair.

'Nik?' She blinked sleepy midnight eyes at him. 'What's happening?'

'I went to get some food.' He rubbed his head ruefully. 'You were asleep and I thought I could kiss you awake.'

'How did that work out for you?'

'I think either you head-butted me or the chair did.'

'Ah, so the old self-preservation kicked in.'

'Yes it would do, because kisses can be deadly. Everyone knows that.'

'Whatcha got in the bags, mister?'

'Fish with green peppers in black bean sauce, Szechuan king prawns, special fried rice and Singapore style noodles.'

Annie perked up instantly. 'Sounds

amazing. I'll get some bowls.' She stood up carefully, and made her way to the kitchen, reappearing with bowls, spoons and chopsticks.

Nik felt relieved to see that Annie looked much better once she'd eaten, and even more relieved to see she steered clear of any more wine and further conversation about soul mates. He wondered if she'd been skipping many meals since he'd been away.

'Are you still up for finishing the tree?' he asked her. 'We only got as far as the lights earlier.'

'Definitely. Can't have an unfinished tree in the middle of December.'

'Let's do it then.' He gathered up the debris of their meal and took it out to the kitchen. She followed with the dirty bowls, and loaded them in the dishwasher.

Together they opened Annie's box of decorations. Because of her love of Christmas, she'd bought a tree decoration from almost every country she'd ever visited — and she and Katie had travelled a lot with their parents over the years. She took out some complicated tasselled decorations from China, hand-painted gourds from New Mexico and her favourite — a Native American dream catcher. There was even a red and gold satin camel from her gap year in India.

'You've collected some lovely tree decorations,' he said, holding a gourd up to admire the delicate painted lizard winding its way around it.

'Katie makes fun of me if she notices a new one.'

'Why would she do that?'

'Because she's my annoying little sister,' she replied with a shrug. 'She lives to torment me, and she thinks I already have more tree decorations than Selfridges.'

'Well she has me to answer to now,' he said.

When the tree had been decorated to Annie's exacting standards, Nik switched on the lights, and they stood back to admire their handiwork. He watched the twinkling lights reflected in Annie's amazing eyes, and couldn't help himself from glancing down at her pendant. Sure enough, it glowed and shimmered with all the colours and lights of the festive season. It was good enough for him.

'It's the best tree ever,' breathed Annie. 'Perfect.'

Nik turned her to face him, and was about to kiss her, when his mobile rang. Muttering threats about the caller, he pulled the phone from his pocket. He didn't recognise the local number.

'Yes?' He said cautiously.

'Mr Knoll?' A deep voice he didn't recognise spoke.

'Yes.'

'This is Ashley Wood Police. We've been alerted that your animals are loose in the road. A pony, a goat and a deer. Two squad cars have been despatched.'

Nik swore loudly. 'I'm on my way.'

'What is it?' Annie grabbed his arm.

'The animals are out. That was the police.'

Annie was already pulling on her

jacket. 'I'll ring Tim.'

Nik gave a horrified look, and she said hurriedly. 'Just in case.'

She switched the tree lights off and they pelted down the stairs and out to Nik's car.

★ ★ ★

When they reached the nursery, there were two police cars with flashing lights across the road blocking any oncoming traffic, and as they parked, Tim drew up behind them in his mud-spattered Land Rover.

'Where are they?' Nik asked the nearest police officer.

'We blocked the road as soon as we could, but the little pony . . . '

'The pony? What happened to the pony?' Annie's voice shook, and Nik put his arm around her. He knew how much she loved the little Shetland.

'He panicked. He's hurt, I think.'

The policeman pointed and Nik pelted down the road with Annie and Tim following.

When they neared Merlin, Nik could see a nasty gash on his withers where the blood was seeping out. Merlin was obviously terrified, and nobody had managed to get near him yet. His coat was matted with sweat and the whites of his eyes showed brightly in the light from the nearby lamppost.

'Annie?' Nik turned to her. 'He likes you the best.'

She nodded, her eyes bright with unshed tears, and she started to walk slowly towards Merlin, crooning softly. His ears flicked at the sound of her voice and he tossed his little head, snorting loudly.

Nik followed her. He listened to her talking quietly to Merlin. She really was incredible with animals.

'It's all right Merlin,' she said. 'We've come to help you. Don't be afraid.' The little pony trembled and danced backwards on his tiny hooves.

'Whoa Merlin, it's only me, it's Annie.' She spoke softly to the frightened pony.

Annie advanced towards him very slowly and managed to grab his leather halter before he took off again.

'Good boy. It's all right.' She stroked his sweating neck and fussed with his ears. He trembled and his flanks heaved. She turned to Tim. 'He's in shock, but I don't think the injury is too bad. He might need a few stitches.'

Nik came back with Gertie and Rudy. Both seemed only too pleased to be caught, and appeared unharmed although obviously scared.

'Let's get them all back in the stable first.' Nik led the way, after thanking the police officers.

'Make sure they're shut in properly next time,' said the Sergeant.

'I did,' said Annie. 'I always do.' She turned to Nik. 'I'm always so careful.'

'I know.' He made sure his tone was reassuring. He believed her of course, but something had gone wrong somewhere. He needed to check the lock on the gate.

Once the animals were safely shut

in the stable, he left Tim and Annie to sedate and treat Merlin, while he went back to assess the scene with the police.

The main gate was always padlocked at night, but tonight the chain swung loose and the padlock was half hidden in the long grass.

'Doesn't look like they were shut in properly tonight.' The Sergeant bent down to pick up the padlock. It was still closed and locked.

Nik picked up the heavy chain. It had been sawn through. He held it out to the Sergeant.

'Looks like this was deliberate,' he said. 'I don't know too many hooved animals that are handy with a hacksaw do you?'

'No need to be flippant, sir,' the Sergeant snapped back. 'Just doing our job.'

Nik apologised. He felt rattled. Who on earth would want to hurt his animals? He didn't have any enemies, did he?

'Can you think of anyone who would want to do this, sir?'

He realised the Sergeant was talking to him again. He shook his head.

'No idea, Sergeant — unless . . . ' He had a sudden horrific thought.

'Unless?'

'We had a problem with an employee who was on a probationary period recently, and she hasn't come back to work since then. But I can't imagine she would be quite this vindictive.'

'You'd be surprised. Come in tomorrow morning and we'll go through everything. First thing please.'

'Of course. And thanks.'

The Sergeant nodded and gestured for his men to leave.

Nik went back up the field to the stable. Annie and Tim were just finishing up. Annie had given Merlin a gentle rubdown with straw, and covered him with his rug, partly to keep him warm and definitely to stop him biting his stitches.

Nik watched her fuss over him and slip a few pony cubes into his manger. She caught him watching.

'He'll be fine now,' she said. 'But I can sit with them tonight if you like?' She turned to Tim. 'Do you think it's necessary?'

'No, they'll be fine with each other,' said Tim giving her an understanding smile. 'Trust me, I'm a doctor.'

'Thanks so much for coming out, Tim.' Nik held his hand out to Tim. 'I really appreciate it.'

The men shook hands.

'All part of our fabulous service,' said Tim. 'You get 'mates' rates' anyway.'

'Thanks again.'

'Do you stable them at night normally?'

'Well, I usually leave the stable door open at night, and leave them to do their own thing,' said Nik.

'Keep them shut in for a couple of nights at least, or until little bitey boy over there has his stitches out.'

'Did he get you? I'm sorry.'

Annie gave a quiet laugh. 'I thought I'd cured him of that.'

'Every animal bites the vet,' said Tim. 'Covered in scars and war wounds I am.'

Wishing them both good night, he picked up his bag, and left.

Annie put her hand on Nik's arm. 'It must have been my fault,' she said quietly. 'I came to feed them, I was the last one here. It must have been me.'

Nik put his hands on her shoulders and gave her a gentle shake. 'Annie, Annie, listen to me. It was *not your* fault. Someone took a hacksaw to the chain on the gate. Deliberately.'

Annie gasped with shock, her eyes huge. 'Why would anyone do that?'

'Why would anyone not notice a three-year-old boy had gone missing and was outside in freezing temperatures, without either coat or supervision?' Nik's tone sounded bitter.

'You think *Lucinda* did this?'

'That would be my guess. Who else do you know with a grudge around here?'

Annie looked back at the animals contentedly eating together. 'If she did this, then she is even more of an evil cow than I thought.'

'I agree,' said Nik. 'Let's shut these guys in and go back to your place shall we?'

'I don't want to be alone tonight,' whispered Annie.

Nik drew her in close. He kissed the top of her head. 'It was never my intention to leave you alone.'

28

17 December

When I woke up on Sunday morning, the first thing I felt was warm. This isn't exactly unusual, although I do have a tendency to wriggle out from under the duvet, and often kick it off altogether, whatever time of year it is. But today, I felt toasty. It could have something to do with the muscular arm flung across my torso, of course.

I turned my head to watch him sleeping. He looked like a Greek God, not that I know many, but he definitely looked how a Greek God should look. I reached out a hand to touch the tousled, corn-coloured hair. It felt silky and soft.

He opened his eyes at that moment, and smiled. 'Hello you.'

'Hey.'

He propped himself up on the arm which wasn't currently draped over me. 'We have to go see the boys in blue.'

'Okay, not exactly romantic.'

'First thing, they said.'

I sighed. 'Do you want to shower first or shall I?'

'You shower. I'll go and make coffee.'

I leaned over to kiss him. 'I told you I love you, right?'

'You did, but I will never get tired of hearing it.'

I watched as he rolled out of bed and pulled on his jeans. I didn't think I'd ever be tired of watching him do that either. With a cheeky wink he sauntered out of the bedroom and made his way to the kitchen.

I took the opportunity to grab some clean clothes and scurry off to the bathroom.

I'd showered and washed my hair, and was getting dressed when Nik tapped on the bathroom door.

'Breakfast is ready.'

'Breakfast? I don't eat breakfast.'

'Well I do, and so should you.'

I opened the bathroom door. 'I didn't even realise I had anything in for breakfast.'

'Come with me.' He crooked a finger at me.

I followed him to my kitchen to find he had indeed found eggs, cheese and half a red pepper, and made a pretty spectacular omelette.

'I'm definitely keeping you,' I told him.

'That was always my evil plan.' He nodded.

'And are you going to tell me more about your evil plan and the soul mate thing today?'

He hesitated. 'Let's get the police stuff out of the way first.'

★ ★ ★

There's plenty of CCTV around our town, and luckily for us, there's CCTV on Nik's road, mainly because it's close to the to the mainline station, and the station car park, I suspect. The cameras showed Lucinda's Audi TT turning into the nursery car park at 10 p.m. and leaving again at 10.30 p.m. The police

214

phoned us at 11.15 p.m. There would have been no reason for her to go to the nursery at that time on a Saturday night, even if she had still been employed there, so she had some explaining to do. Evil witch of a woman. And that was me being complimentary.

We both had to have our fingerprints taken. For me, the whole process felt quite exciting, I really do watch far too much TV. The police assured us it was to eliminate our fingerprints when they dusted the chain and padlock for prints. I felt like I'd dropped into an episode of *Vera* or some other TV police drama.

We left the police station and stopped off to buy a new chain for the paddock gate. Then went on to feed the animals and check on Merlin.

I felt relieved to see Merlin looking much more like his usual perky self this morning. I checked his dressing and made sure the stitches were still intact.

'Tim thinks we should keep him in until the stitches are taken out,' I said. 'But we can let the other two out.'

Nik shooed Gertie and Rudy out in the field, leaving me to explain to a very disgruntled Merlin why he couldn't go with them. I gave him extra pony cubes but he snorted and huffed at them in disgust.

'It's for your own good,' I told him. 'Once your stitches are out, you can go back out in the field.'

I gave him a hug and he batted his white eyelashes at me dolefully.

'Soon,' I promised, dropping a kiss on his velvety nose.

I left him looking after me in a forlorn way, and shut the bottom half of the stable door. Unfortunately at his size, he was too small to look over the top of it, but at least he'd get the fresh air.

'I'll be back later.'

Once outside I noticed Gertie had mountaineered her way onto the top of an upturned oak barrel. Not much wrong with her then. Rudy was following Nik around and butting his arm at regular intervals. Not a lot wrong with him either.

'How's Merlin?'

'Pretty fed up,' I said. 'But he'll be fine.'

I looked over at the gate and could have sworn I saw someone get down from it. But then I have to admit to feeling pretty jumpy at the moment, so I could have just been imagining things.

Nik noticed me looking back over my shoulder at the field and the stable. He linked his fingers through mine.

'We'll come back later and double-check everything. And we'll shut the three of them in for the night. I'll pad-lock the stable door as well.'

'Okay.'

Nik glanced at his watch. 'Pubs are open in a bit. Fancy a drink?'

I gave him a look. 'I'd love a really huge cup of coffee.'

He swung our linked hands. 'Coffee it is.'

29

The coffee shop was cosy and inviting. We managed to grab a table in the corner and were soon sipping appreciatively at mega cappuccinos with deep velvety chocolate stencilled in festive designs on the top.

'Hey look,' said Nik with a mischievous glint in his eyes. 'Holly berries.'

'Don't start.' I grabbed my spoon and scooped up the foamy creation, eating it with relish. 'See? All gone.'

'About Christmas . . .'

I looked up from my coffee. My heart started to pound. I really am awful at serious conversations. 'Yes?'

'Don't look so worried, Annie.' 'I'm just . . .'

He took hold of my left hand in both of his. 'I know. Seriously crap at these kind of conversations.' He grinned.

I pulled a face at him. 'You remember,

huh?'

'I remember everything about you.'

I felt my cheeks flush. Although it was pretty warm and steamy in the coffee shop, so I'm pretty sure that's why I felt suddenly hot. 'Just tell me whatever you want Nik.'

He took a deep breath. 'I'm trying to think where to start . . .'

'Because you're not great at these conversations either,' I said helpfully.

'Well this is a conversation I've never had with anyone . . . ever.'

My heart pounded harder and faster.

'Best to get it out in the open then.'

He looked down at the table for a few seconds, then back at me.

'Did you try to call or text me last week?'

'Loads of times. Especially after Lucinda-Gate. Actually, that's a really good name for her after her latest mean trick, if it was her.'

'It was her, and don't change the subject.'

'Sorry. Yes I did, several times.'

'Did you wonder why I didn't reply?'

'I thought you were somewhere without a signal.' I had no idea where this conversation was going. Forget episodes of *Vera*, we were now in *X-Files* territory. Or maybe even the *Twilight Zone*.

'Your messages only reached me yesterday after I got back.'

'Are you going to tell me why?'

'I'm trying to . . . ' He smiled ruefully. 'This is so difficult. I don't want you to think I'm a raving lunatic.'

'Well I already think that.' I grinned at him. 'But I still like you.'

He let go my hand and leaned back in his chair. I decided he'd carry on when he was ready, so I sipped at my coffee. Whatever the hell he was going to tell me must be deadly serious. I hoped he hadn't killed anybody. He hadn't wanted his fingerprints taken, had he? Perhaps he was a spy. He joked about me being a Russian spy after all.

Lurid, frantic thoughts buzzed manically around in my head, while Nik remained silently staring down into his coffee. I might not be great at serious conversations but I'm even worse at silence, so I decided to break it.

'Hey Nik, you can tell me anything. We've decided we love each other, so from now on — no secrets.'

'You are so special, Annie.' He did look up then, his grey eyes full of warmth. 'Okay, I already asked if you believe in magic, and we kind of established that you don't?'

'Apart from the lights . . . ' My fingers touched the silver reindeer.

'Look at it.'

I looked down and was almost blinded by the dancing lights emanating from the pendant. 'It's gone berserk.' I stared at the colours. 'More than before. Why?'

'The magic is intensified at the moment.' He smiled gently. 'Watch.'

He reached his hand out towards the pendant, and I gasped as thousands of bright sparkles appeared to emanate from his fingertips and flood into the pendant.

'How . . . ?'

He shrugged. 'Magic.'

'Why are *you* magic?'

'My family and I are connected to Christmas.'

I stared at him blankly.

'You couldn't call or text me while I was away, because you need to have a special kind of phone, and because my family home is kind of . . . somewhere else . . .'

'As in an alternate universe or something? Are you an *alien*?'

He did laugh then. 'You watch far too much TV.'

'Not an alien?'

'No. Definitely not an alien.'

'What then?'

I found myself watching his hands for more colourful sparks, but they looked like ordinary hands again. I wondered what was in the coffee. Perhaps I'd become suddenly allergic to coffee or chocolate. Oh that didn't bear thinking about. Surely nobody could cope with being allergic to both coffee and chocolate?

I realised Nik was speaking again.

'Sorry. What?'

'Most of the year, my father and his staff make toys and look after the reindeer on the farm. Does this ring any bells?'

'Sleigh bells, yes.' I nodded. Then I realised what I'd just said, and laughed aloud. 'Oh wait. No. You will not get me to believe . . .'

'I am the only heir.'

'The what?'

'Heir . . . to the . . .'

'Toy business?'

'In a manner of speaking, yes.'

'Uh . . . *huh*.' I looked around the coffee shop, wondering where the cameras were. 'Did Katie put you up to this?'

'Absolutely not.'

'Harry Huckle?'

'Well he has been nagging me since October.'

'To do what?'

'Come clean with you.'

'Why is it so important to tell me in December?'

Nik gave me an approving look. 'My father's — er — special gifts — shall we say, have begun to wane a little. I don't think anything serious will happen for a very long time, probably some years, but if I'm not in a serious relationship soon, the family line could be broken, the magic will start to fade and then things could start to go horribly wrong.'

'Hence the online and speed dating.'

He nodded. 'Yes . . . about that . . . '

I laughed. 'Well, it did look kind of weird in there. I only stopped by to have a go at the idiot who had his dog chained up so tightly it couldn't even sit down.'

'I remember.'

'I reported him.'

'Did they take the dog away?'

'The authorities already have. Anyway, carry on. Who *is* your Dad?'

'I think you have a good idea who he is.'

'Well I know who he *sounds* like. But I don't believe in *him* any more. I'm not five years old.'

'Thank heavens I'm not a vicar then,'

he muttered half to himself. 'Let's go and get some lunch.'

30

Nik thought Annie had coped with his rambling attempts at explaining things pretty well, although he still didn't think she believed him, and he had no idea what to do about that. She chatted normally enough through lunch,buthe noticed she didn't eat much. He wondered again whether she'd been skipping meals during the last week.

'Not hungry then?' he interrupted her chatter about work gently. 'You can talk to me normally, Annie. I'm still me, and I'm really not a lunatic.'

She stopped mid babble, and pushed a thick length of dark hair behind her ear. 'I'm sorry. I went into nervous blether mode didn't I?'

He smiled. 'A little bit.'

'Sorry. I just don't know what to say.'

'Well luckily for both of us, I do.'

She finally gave up on the meal and

pushed the plate away. 'Thank heavens.'

'Annie, will you come and spend Christmas Eve and Christmas Day with me and my family?'

She stared at him, her midnight-blue eyes shining. 'Really?'

'Really.'

'Wow.'

'Is that a yes?'

'Of course.'

'Your parents won't be upset?'

'They'll have Katie and Jon, and I can go round to see them a few days before.'

Without turning his head, Nik suddenly said, 'You can join us for a drink Harry.'

He laughed when Annie turned around quickly to watch the little man making his way over to their table.

'Hello Harry Huckle,' she said, as he sat down. 'Thank you for your help with Lucinda.'

'My pleasure, Annie.' His voice was deep and friendly.

'Annie's going to spend Christmas with us,' Nik said to him.

Harry's walnut-brown face crinkled into a wide smile. 'Now that is really good news, sir.'

Right on cue, Nik's phone rang. He expected it to be his father, except it wasn't. It was the police. He listened to the clipped, efficient tones of the Sergeant, and frowned.

'That's not what I expected,' he said at last. 'But thanks for letting me know.'

He put the phone back in his jacket pocket. Both Annie and Harry were looking at him expectantly.

'No prints on the chain or the padlock — or the gate,' he said. 'So unfortunately, no proof. The CCTV footage isn't admissible as evidence that Lucinda let the animals out, because it only shows her parking her car.'

Annie looked worried. 'Do you think we should stay there overnight?'

Nik smiled and shook his head. 'We'd freeze to death.'

'But whoever they are might come back.'

Nik glanced at Harry, who nodded. 'I

can be there.'

'The animals will be safe, I promise.' Nik touched Annie's hand. 'Harry will make sure of it.'

'Well as long as Harry doesn't freeze to death.' Annie half turned again to look for Harry, but said instead, 'He's gone hasn't he?'

'You learn fast.' Nik raised his glass in a salute.

31

18th December

I spent a long time going over the previous evening's conversation. Nik hadn't actually said aloud what he thought I'd been thinking, or rather who the person was I'd been thinking about. In fact the more I went over the whole evening, the less information he seemed to have given me. I know who his father *sounded* like, but surely that must have been Nik's idea of a joke. I'm grateful he stopped the conversation where he did. I'm not at all sure how the rest of the evening would have gone if he'd carried on.

The invitation to his parents' place for Christmas was exciting nevertheless. I wondered where on earth they could live? Presuming it was on earth. I had a mental picture of an elderly couple in a space ship, then laughed at my own stupid imagination. Wherever they were or weren't, I'd find out on Christmas Eve.

Saying goodbye to Nik again didn't seem so bad this time, especially now I knew we'd be spending Christmas together. Lucinda hadn't returned to the nursery, and Nik had paid her a month's severance pay, which under the circumstances was pretty generous. I still found it hard to believe she would have let the animals out, but I always find it difficult to believe anyone would deliberately hurt an animal. Sadly, facts often prove me wrong. I'm glad I work in the animal care profession and can help put things right — although I do get far too involved sometimes.

Tim came to take out Merlin's stitches the following evening after surgery.

The nasty gash had healed perfectly, and Merlin was back to bucking his way around the field, and baring his teeth at Rudy and Gertie. All back to normal in the paddock then.

'Not a lot wrong with him now,' said Tim with satisfaction. 'He tried to take a chunk out of me several times too, so that's a good sign.' He laughed as

Merlin did a particularly spectacular buck in mid air. 'I think he's happy.'

'He certainly looks happy,' I agreed. 'Do you think I should still shut them in at night?'

'Yes I would do for a while. It's a bit cold for them to be out at night anyway.' Tim checked he had all his instruments back in the bag and closed it. 'Any news on who let them out?'

'We think we know who did it, but there's no proof.'

'Bastards,' Tim said with feeling. 'I hope they get them.'

'Me too. Thanks Tim.'

'No worries. Don't be late in the morning.'

'It's usually the boss who's late.' I punched him on the arm.

We walked across the field together, and even though I knew perfectly well it wasn't my fault the animals got loose before, I felt relieved Tim was there to double check as I locked and secured the gate.

With a cheery wave, Tim got into

his Land Rover and drove off. I leaned against my car, watching Merlin race around the field. Rudy had obviously given up watching him and gone back to eating, whilst Gertie was once again on top of the upturned barrel.

They're fine. They'll be fine. I told myself over and over. Aloud, I said, 'See you later guys.'

It was getting dark, when I went back to feed the animals and bed them down for the night. Frost was already spreading its thick, sparkly blanket over everywhere, and the grass crunched as I walked towards the stable. Unusually, all three of the big animals were waiting by the stable.

'Too cold for you huh?' I said, patting each of them in turn. I unlocked the stable door and shooed them inside. Merlin skittered in first, his little hooves tapping on the stone floor. He went straight in to his stall and peered hopefully in the manger.

'Give me a chance,' I said, laughing.

I soon sorted out their food and water,

and put some extra straw on the floor.

'I'm shutting the door tonight,' I told them. They didn't appear too interested judging from the sounds of contented munching I could hear.

I shut the stable door and locked it with Nik's new padlock. A sound nearby made me turn quickly, and suddenly someone bumped into me so hard, they knocked me off my feet. I hit the frosty frozen ground with some force, bashing my head hard. The fall completely knocked the breath from my body, severely winding me. I attempted to sit up. My breath rasped and burned in my throat, as I tried to breathe normally, whilst waves of dizziness and nausea consumed me.

Whoever the intruder was, they'd sprinted halfway across the field by the time I managed to stand up on very shaky legs.

Then I smelt the fire.

The little shed where Nik kept the feed was on fire. There was an extinguisher in there, I knew that, but I needed to get to it. Grabbing a bucket, I hit the ice on the top of the trough with it, and filled it with freezing cold water. It wouldn't be enough, but it might help me if I couldn't get in the shed to get the fire extinguisher.

Pulling my phone from my pocket, I dialled the emergency services and gave them the address. 'Please hurry.'

Still feeling dizzy and sick, I attempted to wrench the shed door open. The latch felt incredibly hot to the touch, and I knew my hands must be badly scalded, but I had to try for the extinguisher if I had any hope of containing the fire.

In the distance I could hear the sirens, thank goodness — help was coming. I struggled through dense smoke to where the fire extinguisher hung on the wall. Coughing from the smoke, I dragged the hot metal cylinder out into the open. At last it spluttered into action, and I aimed it towards the densest part of the fire.

The sirens were deafening now, and I heard shouting over by the gate. It was still difficult to breath and I coughed violently again until my eyes watered. My head was pounding and I felt desperately ill, but still I continued to aim the extinguisher at the heart of the fire.

Just when I thought all was lost, someone took the extinguisher from me, and strong arms hauled me away from the shed.

There was just time to say, 'Let the animals out,' before I fainted.

★ ★ ★

Waking up in a hospital ward isn't something that's ever happened to me before. They're incredibly white and bright and actually very noisy. Wouldn't you think a hospital ward would be all soothing and quiet?

The first thing I thought of when I woke up was my pendant. Don't ask me why, it just felt very important. The very nice ward sister assured me it was safe, because she'd put it in her desk drawer. When I insisted on wearing it in bed, she obligingly went to fetch it.

'This means a lot to you then?' she said as she fastened it round my neck. 'Not the usual accessory worn with a hospital gown, that's for sure.'

I nodded. My throat still felt as if it was burning from the inside out, and speaking was incredibly painful.

She looked at the pendant. 'It's beautifully made,' she said. 'Strange how it picks up the Christmas lights from our tree, when the tree's right down at the other end of the ward.'

I smiled, my bandaged fingers touching the pendant.

By lunchtime, the police had been, my parents had been and Katie had whooshed in like an avenging angel. My eyes definitely didn't want to stay open any more, and the ward sister had forbidden any further visitors. Actually I didn't think there was anyone left to come and see me. The one person I needed to see more than anything was out of phone contact. I drifted back off to sleep.

The other thing about hospitals is you lose all sense of time. Because there is always someone awake no matter the hour, and the lights, although dimmed at night, are always on. So when I woke up, I didn't really know whether it was day or night and I definitely had no idea what day it was. All I knew was that Nik really had arrived. He sat on an uncomfortable looking chair beside the bed, reading a battered paperback as if he had all the time in the world.

'Nik . . . ?'

He looked up at my croak, and put the book on the bedside cabinet.

'I'm beginning to think you need danger money to look after my animals,' he said, carefully taking hold of my bandaged hand.

'Who's feeding . . . ?' My voice still sounded like Rod Stewart with laryngitis.

'I am. Don't worry, and don't talk.'

'How . . . ?'

'I said, don't talk.' He gave me a mock stern look. 'The animals are fine. The shed isn't. But it's only a shed. Harry told me what happened, and this time we do have proof who the culprit was.'

I took in a breath to ask, but Nik waved a finger to stop me saying anything. 'Luckily for us, the lovely Lucinda took her balaclava off in the car park like she was in a shampoo advert or something, and we can see her face clearly on CCTV.' He laughed. 'I just knew her obsession with her appearance would catch her out someday. And she left plenty of her dainty daubs over the petrol can she brought to start the fire. We have her.'

He leaned over me and stroked my hair back from my forehead. 'Annie, I've never been so scared in my life . . . '

I tried to reach up to touch his face with my other bandaged hand, but discovered I was still attached to tubes.

He brushed his lips over mine. 'They say I can take you home tomorrow.'

I nodded, giving him bandaged thumbs up and a smile.

'Sleep now. I'll be back in the morning.' He kissed me again, and I noticed his soft smile when his glance fell on the pendant.

There was something important I needed to tell him, but I couldn't remember what it was. About Lucinda. But Nik had left.

32

20th December

Luckily for Lucinda, my head was clearer the next day, so I remembered to actually stick up for her. Contrary to what everyone else believed, she hadn't attacked me. In fact she hadn't even meant to bash into me on purpose. I, of all people, should know how easy it is to knock someone over by mistake. I remembered my tissue quest on the day of the wedding, and sending Nik flying in the car park. No matter how badly she'd behaved, I didn't think she'd actually meant to hurt anyone. The fire was another matter. It didn't bear thinking about the consequences if I hadn't been around to get help. And it was nearly Christmas, for heaven's sake. 'Goodwill to all mankind' and all that. I should probably forgive Lucinda in the true Christmas spirit of the season. Maybe she deserved a break?

Badly burned hands and concussion are not exactly my idea of fun, but I had to grudgingly admit that Lucinda probably hadn't done it on purpose. She didn't even know I'd be there. Nik had assured me she would probably only get a suspended sentence for arson, and the mental picture I'd had of her in an unflattering orange prison jumpsuit, walking around a grim quadrangle thankfully faded.

The thought of actually meeting Nik's parents was now beginning to worry me. The closer we got to Christmas Eve, the more worried I became. Katie thought it a hoot that I was going to 'meet the parents' and kept trying to get me to watch the Robert de Niro film with the same title. But I really didn't want to see anyone else's disasters as I felt sure I was perfectly capable of causing my own.

Thankfully, work was keeping me busy, and Nik's menagerie successfully filled the rest of my time. I'd taken to grooming the three bigger animals, who now looked like they could all win a 'best in show' rosette, but I hadn't covered them in tinsel, as Katie predicted I would. I felt sure Merlin would thank me for that, and Gertie would no doubt have eaten the tinsel anyway.

I went out for a pre-Christmas meal one evening with Sally, and spent most of the evening laughing at her stories about the nursery. I thought again how lucky Nik was to have found her — she was definitely a real treasure.

Christmas Eve

When Christmas Eve morning finally arrived, I woke up at literally at the crack of dawn. I peered through my bedroom window to see a light dusting of snow everywhere. It looked so beautiful and magical, sparkling in the cold light of daybreak.

Nik was collecting me at ten. My stomach did a weird kind of lurch. Today I'd find out whether his father was a gangster or . . . well I'd find out everything anyway, like where they lived for a start.

No way would they be living in the North Pole or on a space ship either. I laughed to myself. Nik's hints had done little to tell me anything really concrete. I knew how it all sounded, but I didn't even believe my own thoughts. I hadn't even shared the surreal conversation with Katie. She'd probably have had me committed.

My buzzer sounded at exactly five to ten. I pressed the button, and opened my front door for him. He looked just as gorgeous as always, swooping down to plant a kiss on my lips, and picking up my weekend bag.

'All set?'

'More terrified than set,' I said.

'Don't be. My parents will adore you.'

I didn't have the heart to say what I was actually terrified about, and followed him down the stairs.

Nik's car was parked outside, and I wondered, not for the first time, how far we'd be driving, and how long it would take. I hadn't thought to ask. He put my bag in the boot, and slammed it shut.

I got in the car and fastened my seat belt. Probably needed to be belted in for the long drive to the North Pole or even outer space after all.

Nik pulled away and headed south via the M25. Well, unless we were headed for Heathrow to get on a plane, I didn't think this was the way to the North Pole.

'So how long does it take to get to your parents'?' I turned to look at him. He had an air of excitement about him, which felt infectious.

'Less time than you'd think,' he said.

'Okay, you're starting to spook me a bit.'

'Sorry. Hold on.'

He flicked a switch on the dashboard, and there was a sudden flash of white light.

I think I screamed. I just remember Nik's voice, soothing and deep, telling me everything was all right. It didn't feel all right.

My eyes were screwed tightly shut, and I found myself clinging to the handle on my left. In fact I thought I might never let it go. I could feel myself shaking all over.

'What . . . ?'

Nik continued to talk to me quietly. No wonder he was so good with small children and animals.

'What . . . ?' I said again. My voice had reverted to sounding like Rod Stewart with laryngitis.

Nik reached across and took hold of one of my hands. 'You can let go of the handle, Annie. We've stopped.'

'But *where* have we stopped?' I croaked.

'Open your eyes.'

Reluctantly I opened my eyes to be met with a dazzling bright white light.

* * *

The landscape had completely changed. Instead of the paltry dusting of snow outside my flat, we were parked on a driveway deep in snow, with huge banks of drifted snow on either side.

'What the . . . ?' Third time lucky with the same question.

'Just go with it Annie, it's all good.'

I looked out the car window, and felt my mouth drop open. The snow-laden trees lining the drive were filled with sparkling Christmas lights and the colours reflected from the lights danced across the snow-covered ground. Just like the lights in my pendant. Again.

'Where are we?'

'There's my parents' house.' He pointed.

I could just make out a huge Elizabethan mansion ahead, which nestled amongst more trees decorated with lights.

'Ermm . . .'

He grinned. 'You could say that.'

He started the car again and a few minutes' later we pulled up outside the big oak doors of the house. He eased himself out of the car just as the doors opened.

A small, pretty woman rushed out, followed by at least three dogs that I could see, and a tall, older version of Nik. I breathed out a sigh of relief. So apart from the scary way of travelling here, his parents looked pretty normal.

Nik's mother opened my door as I unclicked the seat belt and pulled me out of the car into a hug.

'Annie, at last!' she said. 'I'm so pleased to meet you.' She kissed me on both cheeks, and I barely had time to say anything before Nik's father swept me up into a bear hug.

'Annie! How marvellous! Welcome, welcome. Come in,' he boomed, and linking his arm through mine, dragged me into the house. 'Bring Annie's bags in Nikolaas.'

It sounded odd to hear Nik being ordered about, and I couldn't resist a grin at him over my shoulder.

The house looked like a piece of ancient history brought to life. An oak-panelled hallway boasted a huge Christmas tree, which went from floor to ceiling and was so exquisitely decorated, I wondered whether it had been professionally done.

I managed, 'I love your tree . . .' before I was ushered into a drawing room, complete with a huge inglenook fireplace, where a log fire crackled. Another huge Christmas tree was set in front of the mullioned windows, and had also been decorated with incredible expertise.

'Have a seat Annie.' Nik's father waved at an armchair by the fire. 'Make yourself at home.'

'Are you hungry?' Nik's mother asked me. 'No, thank you.'

Nik reappeared in the doorway. 'Annie doesn't eat breakfast.'

'She doesn't?'

'Well only if I cook it.'

Nik's father raised his eyebrows. 'You cook?'

'He makes a pretty amazing omelette,' I said.

His mother smiled proudly. 'Of course he does. Can I get you something to drink?'

I thought it might be too early to ask for anything alcoholic, even though I felt the need for something pretty strong.

'Coffee would be lovely,' I said feebly instead. 'Thank you.'

'Might need a dash of brandy in it,'

said Nik with a grin. 'The first journey here is probably a bit of a shock.'

'Ah yes,' his father nodded. 'I forget about the first journey. Brandy is an excellent idea.'

'Erm . . .' I looked from father to son. 'Where exactly is here?'

'I'll show you round after you've had some coffee,' said Nik. 'Then you'll understand.'

Somehow I kept expecting to wake up back at home any minute, or actually, back in hospital. That seemed much more likely. Or perhaps I'd died in the fire, and this was some kind of heaven. Although Nik was here too, so that couldn't be right. But I could still be hallucinating . . .

Nik's mother came bustling back in with four mugs of coffee on a tray.

'Here we are then,' she said.

Nik took the tray from her and put it on a table. He handed a mug to me.

'Drink it slowly,' he advised. 'If Mum's put the brandy in, it will be lethal.'

Lethal sounded quite good to me at

the moment.

I saw Nik's father looking at my pendant a few times.

'Did Wishkin make that for you?' he asked eventually.

'He did,' said Nik. 'I think it's his best work yet.'

'May I?' Nik's father came closer, and I nodded. He held the reindeer gently in the palm of his hand and the lights reflected in his eyes, just like they did in Nik's.

'I think you're right Nikolaas,' his father said softly. 'It is a fine piece of craftmanship.' He winked at me. 'It suits you, Annie.'

'Thank you.' I sipped at my coffee, feeling more and more as if I was in a dream, and I'd wake up any minute. If that was the case, I'm not sure I wanted to wake up just yet. Everything was so beautiful here.

33

Nik said we'd just have time to have a 'quick look around before lunch', and I felt relieved to go and put my coat and boots on, and escape out into the cold snowy grounds.

He took hold of my hand as we closed the front doors behind us and crunched through the snow around the side of the house. When we were out of sight of the house, he pulled me into his arms.

'I'm sorry I didn't warn you about the journey,' he murmured against the top of my head. 'I just felt it would be a bit of an overload of information.'

'So how did we get here — and where exactly is here?'

'Magic,' he whispered with a wink. 'Come on. I'll show you.'

He pulled me towards a huge barn that had bright lights shining from every window.

'Don't tell me, the toy business is in there?'

'Good guess.'

The bright red doors of the barn stood out brightly against all the pristine white snow, and looked like a welcome beacon. Nik pushed the doors open. A cacophony of sound hit me like a wall, but it was nothing to the sight that met my eyes. The place was absolutely cavernous on the inside. I had no idea how it was even possible, and the inside of Doctor Who's TARDIS immediately sprang to mind. The whole place was filled from floor to ceiling with every kind of toy imaginable, and a few hundred more I could never have imagined. From traditional wooden toys and train sets, to the most sophisticated electronic computer games and robots. If this really was *the* Christmas workshop, it was completely amazing. There were hundreds of people running about, shouting orders, carrying out orders, constructing, painting, polishing . . . and they all looked like relatives of Harry Huckle.

I looked up at Nik. 'Wow.' For the second time in a couple of hours, I'd been rendered speechless. Not something that happens to me on a regular basis either.

He looked proud. 'Now you know why I come to help.'

'But there are loads of people working here . . . '

'I don't make the toys, Annie. I come to help with the lists.'

Now I felt a little dense. 'Lists?'

'Of children.'

'So you have to deliver the orders.'

Nik laughed. 'Annie, after all you've seen and everything I've told you, you still don't believe?'

'In what?'

'Christmas is a magical time, and it's my father who keeps it magical.'

'I see. I think.'

He turned me to face him. 'Let me show you the farm.'

We left the workshop, and trudged our way towards the distants table buildings and paddocks.

There in the paddock were eight large

adult reindeer. I brightened up at the sight of the majestic animals. Their hot breath made plumes of steam in the cold frosty air. They turned their handsome heads to look at me, their huge dark eyes assessing me.

'What are their names?' I asked.

'See if you can remember.'

I searched my memory. There was every likelihood Nik's father had named his reindeer after Santa's famous reindeer.

'Dasher, Dancer, Prancer . . . Rudolph . . . '

'Rudolph isn't here. He's usually in the other paddock with his mate, what with him being the king and all. My Rudy is his son.'

'So . . . '

'So . . . Dasher, Dancer, Prancer, Vixen, Comet, Cupid, Donner and Blitzen.'

'Your Dad really did name them after Santa's reindeer then.'

Nik frowned slightly. 'I thought once you were here, you'd believe . . . '

'Nik I would really love to believe in Santa, and the magic of Christmas, and I have to admit that here it almost feels possible . . . '

'What about the journey here?'

'Actually, I think I might still be unconscious in the hospital . . . '

'Your logic is quite frightening sometimes.'

I looked down at my pendant. The coloured lights glowed incessantly now. In fact the pendant glowed more and more with every passing minute we were here.

To give myself something to do, I walked over to the fence and started talking and petting the reindeer. They crowded around me and I felt Nik watching.

I turned around and the look on his face filled me with a warmth that I've never felt before.

'Do you know how many people those reindeer allow to pet them other than my father, my mum and myself?'

I ran my hand down the glossy sleek

neck of the closest reindeer. 'Probably quite a few?'

'Nobody.'

'*Nobody?*'

'Nope. Reindeer are strange creatures, and these reindeer are very special. They have a very important job to do.'

'So if your father has to deliver all over the world in one night — and I'm not saying I believe he does — how is it possible?'

'How was it possible for us to get here in minutes?'

'Magic?'

'*Now* you're getting it.'

'So how come your dad doesn't look like Santa?'

'You'll be here when he leaves tonight, and you'll see that by then he will look like Santa.'

'How? Oh no, don't tell me . . . *magic*.'

'See how easy it is when you try.'

I laughed. Actually I didn't really care whether he was winding me up or not — I loved him and I loved being with him. This place felt magical, and if I was honest, it looked just like every glossy Hollywood Christmas movie I'd ever seen that had Santa in it.

'Just tell me this isn't a film set.'

'It isn't a film set, and again, I'll remind you about the journey here.'

'Magic is real,' I whispered.

'Very real.'

'So one day . . .'

'I'll take over from my father.'

'Will you have to be hugely fat with a white beard and shout 'ho ho ho' all the time?'

He moved closer and wrapped his arms around me. 'Where were you when I said about Dad changing his appearance with magic, before he goes out on deliveries?'

'So later tonight he really is going to look like Santa?' I couldn't even believe I was asking this question.

Nik kissed the tip of my nose. 'You'll have to wait and see won't you?'

34

After a huge meal, we all went to sit in the sitting room by the roaring log fire. 'I understand you met our reindeer, Annie.' Nik's father smiled across at me. 'What's your professional opinion of them?'

I remembered stroking their glossy coats and looking into the huge shining eyes.

'I'm not an expert on reindeer,' I said. 'But yours are spectacular in my humble opinion.'

He looked pleased. 'Thank you, that's wonderful to hear.'

Nik's mother glanced at the old grand-father clock across the room, 'Don't forget the time,' she said.

'Thank you my dear.' He stood up and grinned back at me. How like Nik's grin it was too. It was infectious and made it absolutely impossible for me not to smile back. 'Will you excuse me Annie? I have

259

to get ready for the deliveries.'

'Of course.'

I wondered whether this would be the moment when Nik and his family shouted the festive equivalent of 'April Fool' at me, but nothing happened. I felt Nik's eyes on me and turned to look at him. He merely winked and sat back in his chair.

A sleek black cat wandered in and leapt nimbly onto Nik's lap. None of the three dogs currently lying in a big furry heap together by the fire even raised an eyebrow at the feline intruder.

'Your dogs don't mind the cat?' I watched the cat make itself comfortable, and then close its fluorescent green eyes in bliss.

'Most of the animals get along here,' he said. 'Apart from Rudolph, who likes to rule the roost of course.'

'Far too full of himself that reindeer,' said Nik's mother. 'Especially on Christmas Eve.'

I could believe anything was possible sitting in this beautiful room. The moving shadows from the firelight flickered on the wood-panelled walls while the multi-coloured sparkling lights from the Christmas tree shone out from their corner, bathing the whole room in a warm festive glow.

'This room is so lovely . . .' I started to say, when the door flew open.

There stood . . . well . . . *Father Christmas*. There was no other name for the large jolly man standing there. Except for Santa Claus, Kris Kringle, St Nicholas — just to name a few — so actually there are quite a few other names for him.

There he stood, dressed in a bright red suit and hat trimmed with white, large black shiny boots, and sporting a flowing white beard. This man no longer looked like Nik's father. If indeed he was Nik's father.

I felt conscious that I was gawping, and put a hand over my mouth to hide the gawp. Nik chuckled quietly from his armchair, and I felt someone tap my shoulder. Nik's mother rubbed my arm in a sympathetic way.

'It's a bit much to take in all at once dear,' she said kindly. 'Nikolaas has never brought anyone home before, so he's not very good at avoiding the . . . surprise of it all.'

'I did my best,' Nik protested. 'Annie thought I was joking.'

'Ermmm . . .' It was the best I could manage, and appeared to be my new favourite word.

Nik stood up, unceremoniously waking the cat, who landed on all four paws on the floor, only to immediately leap back onto Nik's chair and curl up.

'I'm sorry Annie. My revelation wasn't very revealing was it?'

I took a deep breath but closed my mouth before I could say 'Ermmm' again.

Nik's father laughed from the doorway. It didn't sound like 'ho ho ho' but it was close. 'Come outside everyone and wave me off.'

This I had to see. Somehow I knew this would be the moment.

We all trooped outside. There was no sleigh and no reindeer. A wave of disappointment ran through me. Had it all been some kind of hoax after all?

Then I heard them. Sleigh bells. The tinkling sound carried sharply and beautifully on the cold night air. Flurries of sparkling snowflakes began to fall, and suddenly I believed in the impossible.

Rudolph came into view first, his nose glowing red, just like every Christmas card with reindeer I have ever seen. Harry Huckle was leading him, with a proud smile on his face.

The other reindeer obediently followed their leader, the huge sleigh drifting effortlessly behind them. I truly had never seen a more amazing sight. A tiny part of me still wondered whether I might be lying unconscious in hospital, but then I felt Nik's arm around my waist, and when I looked up at him, I knew everything was real.

We watched Nik's dad climb aboard the laden sleigh and take up the reins. 'I'll see you all tomorrow,' he called.

'Enjoy your evening.'

From a shake of the reins, the reindeer trotted off, and were airborne for just a moment before they disappeared altogether in a flurry of snowflakes and sparkles.

'Gone,' I said faintly.

Nik hugged me close. 'Yes, gone for now.'

I stared upwards at the space where the reindeer and the sleigh had disappeared. All I could see now was the falling snow against the velvety night sky.

'What if you hadn't met me?' I turned to face Nik.

'We could have lost the magic of Christmas altogether.'

I looked up at him. 'Magic is real,' I said.

'Magic *is* real,' he agreed. 'And Christmas is the most special time of the year.' He leaned down to kiss me, and his eyes glinted and sparkled with the same dancing lights that shone like a beacon from my pendant.

*Other titles in the
Linford Romance Library:*

THE OTHER WOMAN

Wendy Kremer

Matthew faces a tough choice. Should he quit his job and take on the family firm? His girlfriend in London, Celia, definitely can't imagine living in the provinces, but Matthew knows the local community depends on the company for work. One of its employees, Kate, unintentionally helps him to accept the challenge. Kate likes Matthew, but he already has a partner, so he's off-limits. Will Matthew yield to Celia's demands?

LA VIE EN ROSE

Denise Robins

Heiresses twice over, Viola and her young sister Giselle travel to exotic Khartoum to be with their guardian, the sophisticated Lionel. However, Viola's excitement is spoiled by her sister's obvious infatuation with Lionel — and the presence of Ted, a determined suitor. Violently objecting to a marriage between Ted and Viola, Lionel proposes himself — and she accepts. But Ted is vengeful, and knows of Lionel's financial affairs. Can Viola really be sure whether Lionel loves her — or her money . . . ?

MERRY MISTLETOE

Emma Davies

Sherbourne Mistletoe has been prized and sold at the annual Mistletoe Fair for over a century. But could this year possibly be the last? With her father's sudden death, and debts mounting up, it looks as though Freya's only hope for the future is to sell her beloved family home. Then the arrival of the mysterious Amos Fry brings a glimmer of hope — and Freya might just fall in love with Christmas all over again.

A DAUGHTER'S CHRISTMAS WISH

Victoria Cornwall

Christmas, 1919. A promise to a fellow soldier leads Nicholas to Cornwall for Christmas, and to the teashop managed by Rose: the youngest daughter of a family whose festive spirit has been blighted by their wartime experiences. But as Nicholas strives to give Rose the best Christmas she could wish for, he begins to question whether his efforts are to honour his friend — or if there is another reason . . .

UPSATIRS, DOWNSTAIRS

Alice Elliott

Rumours are flying around the servants' quarters at Brackenfold Hall. Items are going missing, and nobody knows who to trust anymore. Fingers start pointing at Bess, the sullen new scullery maid — but housemaid Sally Halfpenny feels sure she isn't to blame. Sally vows to uncover the true identity of the thief. Meanwhile, a fever has hit the whole village, and she fears for the safety of her parents. Not to mention the anguish of her unrequited love for footman James Armstrong . . .